MW01633645

PROTECTING TALIA (SPECIAL FORCES: OPERATION ALPHA)

LOVED BY THE SEAL
BOOK THREE

JULIA BRIGHT

Dear Readers,

Xoxo

Susan Stoker

Zip tossed back the last of his beer and stood. Disillusionment filled him and settled with the disappointment burning in his belly. So he was alone. Big deal. It wasn't like he wanted a relationship. The bitterness on his tongue wasn't jealousy. He'd vowed to never settle down, and he wouldn't break his vow. But seeing both Trip and Hop happy, along with their buddies Kevlar, Safe, and Blink, made him want something more. Having a woman in his bed, someone who got him, who could laugh with him, would make him feel good.

No. He couldn't do it. Getting involved with someone was a complication he couldn't afford.

Thoughts of his last long-term relationship

invaded, twisting up his guts. It had ended in disaster shortly before he joined the Navy. Heck, she might have been the reason he joined up. Being a part of the Navy had been a great decision, probably the best he'd ever made. But the turmoil she'd unleashed in his life had almost taken him down so hard he wouldn't have recovered. He would never settle down again.

He headed to the back hall and was about to enter the gents when the door for the ladies' room opened and a woman with dark hair poked her head out. Their gazes met and panic filled her face for a second, then the door slammed and she was gone.

What was that about? He took care of business, and while washing his hands, he heard a faint yell. It wasn't a scream from a guy. No, that shout was from a woman. Why was a woman yelling?

He stepped out into the hall, trying to figure out where the noise had come from. No one seemed excited in the main room of the bar. Maybe one of the waitresses had shouted something. He wasn't sold on that conclusion, though.

He shook his head, pushing away the worry. He didn't know what was going on, but it wasn't any of his business.

He took two steps and paused when something banged hard against the other side of the ladies' room door. Zip stalled, waiting for the door to open. Nothing happened.

When he heard a muffled yell, he knew he had to go in. On missions, he didn't hesitate when entering women-only spaces. Here in the US, he knew he could get in trouble. But from the noise coming from the other side of that door, there seemed to be a problem.

"Coming in!" he yelled as he pushed the door open.

The sound of struggling grew louder. He stepped in, seeing a woman on the ground trying to push away the man on top of her. The jerk punched her, but lucky for her, he hadn't gotten a good wind-up. It had to have hurt, but she hadn't passed out.

Zip moved fast, hauling the guy off the woman. He had one hand on the dude as he yanked the door open and shoved him out into the hall. Stepping into the ladies' room had garnered the attention of two men who grabbed the jerk he'd pulled off the woman. Confusion filled their faces, and Zip pointed at them.

"Don't let him get away. He was punching a woman in here."

"What the fuck is going on?" the woman he'd seen tending bar yelled as she squeezed past the two big guys holding the jerk against the wall.

Zip grunted. "He was beating up someone in here. Have you called for an ambulance?"

The bartender shook her head. "Fuck. I don't need this kind of shit."

Neither did he. But here he was dealing with it. He stepped into the bathroom and froze as he stared down into the bluest eyes he'd ever seen. She'd sat up and was rubbing her jaw, which looked red and angry. The desire to help her grew, and he was about to move closer when the bartender started yelling.

"Fuck! What did you do, you stupid girl?"

The woman with blue eyes blinked up at the bartender. Fear, or something like it, filled her face as she shook her head. "Nothing."

Zip glanced from the bartender to the woman still on the floor. What the hell was going on? Why was this woman acting like the person who'd been beaten up was in the wrong?

The bartender pointed at the woman on the

ground and sneered. "Get the fuck out and don't come back. I don't need you causing problems."

Zip wanted to step in, but it seemed like these two knew each other. Their reactions were too wild to be strangers. The bartender was pissed, and the woman on the ground was frightened. He'd seen a lot of bad actors as a Navy SEAL. Maybe this woman in the bathroom was a horrible person and deserved the anger thrown her way. He didn't think so, though.

Zip wasn't known for being quiet. He'd been told over and over again to zip it. After years of being told to shut up, he tried to keep his nose out of other people's business, but he couldn't let this go. "Want me to call the police, or maybe someone to come help?"

The woman he'd helped with the bluest eyes he'd ever seen shook her head as she stood. "No. Wouldn't do any good, anyway."

Zip didn't understand the situation. She'd been beaten up in the bathroom of this bar, and he'd pulled that guy off her, but everyone was acting like she was in the wrong. She moved to squeeze past him, but he grabbed her arm and held on. Her gaze shot to his, and a murderous look filled her eyes.

"Let go."

"Only if you can tell me that you are okay." She didn't look okay. The cut on her forehead was deep, and her jaw was already swelling.

She pressed her lips together, and he swore he saw more than just anger in her expression. "Why do you care?"

He held her gaze as he answered. "It's what I do."

"Both of you get out, or I'll kick you out!" the mean bartender bellowed before turning around to leave.

Zip rolled his eyes. "Seriously, what is her problem?"

The woman standing next to him huffed out a breath. "That's my sister."

Her words brought Zip up short. How could one sister treat another like this? He wanted to tell the bartender to stop being such a jerk, but obviously they had a history, and he was sure nothing he said would change her attitude.

2

Talia Mast should never have come to the bar, even if it would benefit Cheryl. Her sister was the worst type of narcissist. She'd turned everyone against Talia, even their parents. Why should she care if someone wanted to do something bad?

"Hey, wait up."

Talia turned and rolled her eyes at the man who'd come into the bathroom to save her. Little did he know she wasn't worth saving. Maybe he wasn't there to save her. He could be working with her sister. "Did she send you out here to beat me up this time?"

A look of shock crossed his face. "No!"

At least he had the decency to look and sound

offended. She put her hand on her hips and cocked them to the side as she tilted her head. "Give it time, and she'll have you eating out of her hand."

"No, she won't. You need help. Let me at least take care of that wound on your head."

Talia reached up and winced as she wiped the dirt and grime off her forehead. But it wasn't grime or dirt, it was blood. "Bastards."

He took a step closer and spread his hands, making him appear innocent. "Let me look at it and help you."

"What are you, some kind of doctor?"

"No, but I know how to take care of a wound. Let me just look. I have a kit in my trunk."

She shook her head and scoffed. "So you drive around with some kind of medical kit in your car just looking for people to fix up? That sounds suspicious. What are you, some kind of serial killer?" When he rolled his eyes, she couldn't help but laugh. "You look like a dork when you roll your eyes with that beard."

"Well, I am a dork, so at least you got that right."

Laughter spilled out, and she shook her head. The pain made her stop moving, and she groaned. "I bet you say that to all the girls."

He moved to her and put his hand on her back as he gently guided her to his car. She should make a run for it. Cheryl could have paid him to kidnap her. She wouldn't put it past her sister.

"Why are you helping me? Talking to me will get you banned from that bar."

"It was a shitty bar. Not my usual place. I needed time to think away from friends."

"If I had friends, I sure as shit wouldn't abandon them. You might be worse off than I am."

He grunted, disgust crossing his face. "It's not like that."

"What is it like, then?"

"Let me fix that bloody mess first, then we can talk."

"Fine. I don't need it dripping on my beautiful dress." She curtseyed, holding out an imaginary skirt. Her gray t-shirt was already stained from stuff that had happened earlier. A little more blood wouldn't make that much difference.

The guy opened his trunk, and she glanced in, seeing he had multiple bags in there. No way would he have room for her in there. Unless he folded her up really small.

"You just get back from a trip?"

He shook his head. "Nope. Just need to take some things to work with me."

"What kind of work?"

His lips thinned, and he met her gaze. "Navy. Now be quiet."

She nodded. "What's your name? Figure I need to know since you're all up in my business."

"Zip."

"Zip? Are you trying to tell me to shut up?"

He shook his head. "No. Call me Zip. That's what I go by."

She narrowed her eyes, not believing a word he was saying. Maybe he didn't want to tell her his name. "Do you have another name?"

His lips turned down in a deeper frown under his mustache and beard. "I told you mine. Now you tell me yours."

Was he trustworthy? She had no clue. She'd come to her sister because she knew some shit and wanted to help, but Cheryl had once again proven that blood was the thinnest substance on earth. "It's Talia. That was my sister, Cheryl. You should probably stay clear of her. She won't like that you helped me. Like I said, you'll be banned."

He shrugged like he really didn't care. "That's okay. It was a shit place, anyway."

"Tell me your real name."

"Lewis."

"Really?"

"Yeah, first name is Lewis. Zip fits me better."

She snorted a laugh, and embarrassment filled her. He probably thought she was a real dork. Heck, she was a total mess. Might as well add dork to the list.

He opened the bag and pulled out some supplies. "I need to clean you up before I put the antiseptic on. It's not too bad. Maybe one stitch."

"Can you give stitches?"

He nodded and met her gaze. "Yes. But I won't use stitches, really. I'll use some medical glue before I use stitches."

"Great. Now you're going to be gluing my head closed."

"I sure am. Now be quiet so I can work."

"You're bossy, aren't you?"

"Yeah. Now zip it so I don't make a mistake. Your face moves when you speak, and I don't want to mess anything up."

She studied him as he worked, taking in his brown eyes that were kind, and his lips that thinned as he worked on her. He had a good tan and though he looked serious, she could see kindness in his eyes.

It had been a while since anyone had looked at her with kindness. She was used to getting the worst from people.

"Almost got you cleaned up enough to see that indeed, you do need some glue on that. If I was doing stitches, it would be at least three. We could go to the hospital if you feel better about it."

"No. Dickwad is working tonight."

Zip's eyebrows shot up. "Dickwad?"

"Richard. He's my ex. I caught him fucking my sister."

Zip didn't say anything, but he leaned back and caught her gaze for a few seconds. When he went back to fixing her up, his lips thinned, and she could tell he was concentrating hard.

"This may hurt a little."

"Why would gluing my head closed hurt?"

"I'm going to have to push the edges together and line up the skin so it doesn't pucker. I'd like to leave you without a scar."

"Do you think a scar would make me look like a badass?"

He leaned back and lifted his brows. "You already look like a badass. You don't need any help in that department."

She laughed, and he rolled his eyes, so she

laughed more. He grunted and frowned, but she could tell it was playful. This felt so freaking good, laughing and talking with someone. It had been a while.

"Be quiet. I need to work."

She went quiet, staring at the spot where his shirt was open at his neck. His beard was neatly trimmed, and he'd shaved his neck, leaving a hard line under his chin. He wasn't wearing cologne, but he didn't smell bad. There was a slight hint of something like sandalwood, but it wasn't overpowering. It was probably his soap. A tuft of hair poked out from his open collar, making her want to investigate just how hairy he was.

His shoulders were broad, and she bet he was packed with muscles. The way he'd dealt with the guy inside meant he was strong. Cheryl didn't employ weaklings and when the bouncer had gone up against Zip, Cheryl's employee appeared to be small and weak.

Why had she come to see Cheryl? She knew her sister was an asshole. She'd worked to ruin Talia's life before. She should have known better than to come here to warn her sister, but she couldn't help herself.

3

Zip liked this woman. She was funny. He bet she wouldn't put up with bullshit. What was up with her sister? There were two sides to every story, and he needed more information to understand what was going on. But from what he'd seen from Talia, she wasn't a bad person.

"I like how it's lined up. You could go to a doctor, but I have to say I did a great job."

"I'll be the judge of that. Let me see a mirror."

"How about a phone? I'll turn the camera around."

He held up the phone, and she gasped. "I look like shit."

He shrugged. "I've seen worse."

Her nose wrinkled as she stared at him. "Gee, thanks."

His lips twitched into a smile before he schooled his expression. "How are you getting home?"

She clicked her heels together, then shrugged. "Well, that didn't work. I guess I'll walk."

Her reference to *The Wizard of Oz* made him chuckle. He wasn't going to let her walk, though. Not after what had happened to her. "I'll drive you."

She clasped her hands together and opened her mouth in shock. "Really?"

He nodded, feeling like he was about to get blasted by her. "Yes, really."

She snorted and looked at him like he was rotten meat. "I'm not getting in a car with a stranger. What kind of fool do you think I am? I mean, I'm obviously a fool because I came here to see my sister, but I'm not the type of fool who gets into some stranger's car."

"We aren't strangers now. I know your name, and you know mine. We're practically family."

"Oh, hell no. My family would just as soon see me dead as alive."

"Okay, we're not family. We're two people who just met, but I can't let you walk home. Not after seeing that guy hitting you. You can send a text to a friend and let them track you."

Talia scoffed. "Cheryl made sure I don't have friends. There is no one who would care if you dumped me on the side of the road."

Anger rose up inside, but he held it in check. "Fine." Zip pulled out his phone and called Trip. "Hey, can you send me Ellis's number? I have someone who needs a ride, but she needs someone to send her location to."

"Sure. I'll text it."

He liked how his buddies just trusted him and didn't ask questions. They were solid, and he knew they had his back, even in something small like this. "Thanks, man." He ended the call and met her gaze.

"Wait. I don't know this Ellis person. How can I trust him?"

"Ellis is a woman, my friend's woman. You have to get home, and your sister is dangerous. Trust Ellis. Here, call her and tell her you need someone to know you're with me and that you want someone tracking your location."

TALIA GRABBED her phone and entered the number from Zip's screen. A woman answered immediately.

"Hello."

"Zip said you'd track my location. Why should I trust him?"

"Trip said you'd call. I'm Ellis."

"I'm Talia."

"You can trust Zip. He won't harm you. He'll take you home and make sure your place is safe."

"Doubt it."

"No, he will."

How could she explain the hell her family had put her through? It wasn't normal at all and people didn't understand. "It has nothing to do with him. My place will never be safe. I could have police sitting outside my door, and I'd still be in danger."

"Oh, I'm sorry. Did something happen?"

"My family. They aren't nice."

"That sucks. Well, Zip is a good friend. Maybe your luck is changing."

"I'm not going to hold my breath."

"He'll make sure you get home. And Talia, give me a call this weekend, maybe we can get a drink."

She didn't know what to say for a second. Why would this complete stranger want to get a drink with her? The offer honestly shocked her, and she had no excuse lined up for why she couldn't join this woman for drinks. "That would be nice. Thank you."

The second the call ended she wondered if she'd made a mistake. Friends didn't stick around once her family got to them. Maybe getting this person involved was wrong. Ellis didn't know what kind of hell her family started.

She shoved her phone into her pocket after sending tracking information to Ellis's number. When she looked up and met Zip's gaze, a shiver slid through her. What was that look about? No way would this man be interested in her. Besides, he wasn't like the guys she usually went for. But what good had that done for her? The last man she'd been serious with had ended up stabbing her in the back by sleeping with Cheryl.

She had the feeling that this man in front of her wouldn't fall victim to Cheryl's lies. She could trust Zip. Maybe it was the way he held her gaze, or just something deep inside, but he didn't seem like the type to bend to her family. He would tell them to go to hell.

"Okay. I'll let you take me home."

"Good. Get in, and you can give me your address."

"You won't come to track me down and stalk me like some weirdo and make me regret this?"

"No. You don't ever have to see me again unless you want to."

She slid into the passenger seat and looked up, meeting his gaze. "What if I want to see you again?"

ZIP DIDN'T WANT to make too much of her words, so he shrugged, but his chest grew warm as he thought about seeing Talia again. He shut her door and moved around the car, trying to cover his feelings. He was confused. This woman was sassy and strong, but she had a streak of vulnerability he spied when she talked about her family. What was up with that?

He followed the directions, getting on the freeway after a few turns. "I don't want to make you think I'm better than I am. I would never do anything with someone who wasn't into what we were doing, but I've never been the type of guy who was in it for a long time. I'm not good enough for you."

Talia scoffed. "You obviously don't know what you're talking about."

He glanced at her, seeing her frown. "What do you mean by that?"

"I'm trash and I know it. I'm no prize."

Anger flashed. "You shouldn't talk that way about yourself."

She snorted. "Then neither should you."

He huffed, trying to come up with something to say. It was hard to argue with her while driving. Why was he even arguing with her about this? She was someone he'd just met, not someone he would ever see again.

Laughter from Talia was the last thing he expected. "Oh man, you're so mad because I'm right. I bet you're a cinnamon roll."

He cut his gaze her way then focused on the road. "What?"

"You know, one of those guys who is all sweet and gooey in romance books. The kind of guy who would be supportive."

Her words made his heart hurt. Back before the Navy, he might have been that kind of guy, but now he never let anyone get close. "I'm not. I'm an asshole."

"Well, asshole, I bet that's an act. You're too sweet and kind."

He exited the freeway and the map directions told him to turn. Her place was only a few yards after another turn, so he didn't have much time with her. Anger slid through him. He had to show her he wasn't sweet. He was a total dick. He didn't want her to think he would be the type of man who would stick around. He was nothing at all like a cinnamon roll, whatever that was.

When he stopped the car and cut the engine, he hopped out and moved around to the passenger side before she could get the door open. He helped her up and slammed the door, then pushed her up against the side of the car and braced his hands on the roof beside her shoulders.

She looked up at him, her blue eyes tinged with boredom. He had to prove to her that he was a dick. He wasn't sweet and gooey. He was harsh and terrible.

He leaned in, his lips less than an inch from hers. "I'm dangerous and mean. I'm not good," he said with as much of a growl as he could muster.

Her fingers flitted over his chest, then traced down to his belly, sending fireworks through him. Being this close to her felt like an out-of-control car speeding down the freeway that was about to crash. When her tongue came out and licked at his lips, he jerked back as heat filled him.

She giggled as she ducked under his arm and escaped his cage. He turned and watched as she raced up the stairs to the crap apartment above an Italian restaurant he'd never been to before. He wanted to follow her, but if he did, he feared he would show her he was a total cinnamon roll, and she would never let him live it down.

4

T alia stared at her reflection in the mirror. She looked like shit. There was no way anyone as good-looking as Zip would ever be interested in her. If he ever found out what she'd done, he'd never talk to her again.

She turned away from the mirror and ran the towel over her hair. "Ouch."

Zip had covered the glue with a clear bandage so she could wash her hair, but when she accidentally touched the area, pain blossomed. She would have to watch how much she poked the spot over the next few days. The bruising would get her in trouble at work, but what could she do?

She'd gone to her sister because when she dropped her car off for service, she'd been at the right place to hear that someone wanted to do a hit on the bar. Of course, Cheryl hadn't believed her. It served her right for trying to help. No one from her family was even halfway decent. They'd all turned away from her when she'd been a teen, and Cheryl convinced them to believe the worst about her.

She let go a growl in frustration. "Of course, he doesn't want me. It has to be some kind of act. Maybe he's working for Cheryl." She snorted, angry at herself for liking the guy. She knew better than to trust anyone.

Leaving San Diego was in the works, but every time she got close, something happened. Getting involved with a man like Zip would keep her here, and she didn't want to be in this area any longer.

Her phone pinged, and she glanced at it, seeing the first few words of the message. Her sister had gotten a new burner phone.

Text: *You're going to pay!*

Talia squeezed her fists and closed her eyes. She really didn't know why her family was so awful. There wasn't a name signed on the message, but she knew it was Cheryl. Every time she blocked one phone number, a few days later, she'd get a text from a new number. She wished she had enough time in the day to pester her sister, but she had work, and though she wasn't getting anywhere with it, she was trying. It was almost too hard to keep moving forward, but she wasn't ready to give up yet.

When Ellis texted her the next day, she thought about not replying, but she wanted to see Zip again. She didn't doubt she was making a mistake, but when had she ever made great decisions?

After she texted Ellis back, her phone rang. She answered on the first ring. "Hello."

"It's Ellis. Would you be okay getting together for coffee on Saturday morning?"

She didn't hesitate. "Sure. That would be great." She wanted to slap her forehead for answering so quickly and sounding desperate. No question, she was ruining any chance she had with Zip. Ellis would report back to Zip, telling him how desperate she sounded. For once, she wished she could be cool and calm.

"Awesome. I saw you aren't too far from where we live. How about we meet at Java House?"

"Sure, I love that place."

"Is nine good?"

"I'll be there on Saturday morning at nine. Thank you."

"Of course. I'm looking forward to getting to know you."

The call ended, and Talia leaned against the wall, wondering if she was making a mistake. If Cheryl ever found out she was making friends with these people, she would do whatever she could to poison them against her.

Maybe this time she could have something for herself. The key was to keep her family from finding out that she had friends. But that was easier said than done.

ZIP STILL FELT the tingle from Talia licking his lips. The quick flick of her tongue had shocked him. He'd been dumbfounded by the bold move. Maybe he was a cream puff or whatever she'd called him. He wanted to drop everything and do whatever she needed.

"Zip, what are you doing?" Q yelled from in front of him.

"Shit, sorry." He grabbed the rope and tied it off. Luckily, he wasn't doing anything dangerous. Still, it was shitty of him not to be one hundred percent present for this exercise. If he didn't get it together, he would get someone hurt.

"What's your deal?" Rider asked a little later.

"It won't happen again." He hated being called out for having his head up his ass. Everyone he knew suffered from being distracted at some point in training. Still, it wasn't an acceptable excuse.

Trip came over and tapped him on the back. "What's got your mind working overtime?"

"It's nothing."

Bud snorted. "It doesn't sound like nothing. Let me guess, you met someone."

"No." He sounded way too defensive. They all knew he was lying. He needed to get his shit together and keep it together so they had no reason to call him out. Now, he was telling them half-truths. That wouldn't work in their environment. Dealing honestly with these guys was the only way to go, but there wasn't anything with Talia—not really.

Q snorted. "Well, if she's as good-looking as you are distracted, then she's a looker."

Zip shook his head. "There isn't anyone."

"That's a lie," Q said.

Zip pressed his lips together and shook his head. "I'm not dating anyone."

Q tipped his water bottle at Zip and narrowed his gaze. "But there is someone you're interested in."

Zip didn't want to talk about this right now. He would catch hell for his prior statements about never settling down.

Trip held his gaze, his eyes narrowing slightly. "Let's get back to work."

Zip wanted to thank Trip, but he was trying not to bring attention to his calling Trip for Ellis's help. He didn't want the guys asking questions yet. They would have enough questions once word got out that he'd met someone he wanted to get to know. There wasn't any crime in that. They weren't even dating. In fact, he wanted to prove to her that he wasn't a marshmallow. He was a badass who couldn't be trusted.

5

Talia felt giddy walking into the coffee shop. No one had ever invited her to coffee, and no one polite had ever wanted to hang out with her. Her family had done a number on her.

She pushed away thoughts of the crap in her past and looked for the woman wearing the green t-shirt. She spied a woman sitting in the corner, and her stomach dropped. Ellis looked like she had her shit together. Her dark hair and pale skin made her look elegant, and Talia was anything but elegant.

"Oh, Talia." Ellis waved from her seat and stood, moving to her.

Talia froze. Was this woman connected to her

family? There was no way. Her family didn't know everyone, or did they?

Ellis pulled her into a hug. She sucked in a sharp breath, trying to figure out what was going on. Ellis leaned back, not giving any indication she'd noticed Talia's stiffness or the ugly bruises and cuts she'd gotten from the beating.

"I'm Ellis. It's nice to meet you. I'm so glad I could help you. I ordered a latte for you. I hope that's okay."

Talia would normally turn on the snark, but this wasn't her family or their friends. "Thank you."

"I also got a few scones. I love scones. Have you ever been to England?"

Talia shook her head. "No. I've hardly left San Diego."

"Well, these scones aren't as good as what you get in England, but they are okay." Ellis flashed a smile. "Come sit. We can chat over there."

Talia nodded, hoping she could recover and have a normal conversation without being snarky and offending Ellis. No way would Zip want her in his life. She was hard edges and vinegar, and Ellis was sweetness and sugar. She could never compete with someone like this.

Ellis took a seat just as their coffees came. The

scones were round, and there was jam and something else on the table that Ellis indicated was for the scones.

She wasn't sure, but Ellis seemed to notice how uncomfortable she was and picked up a scone, showing Talia what to do. She felt absolutely out of her depths. No question that her upbringing had severely lacked key activities that would help her know how to act in this situation.

She mimicked Ellis's actions and took a bite of the scone. It was decent. A bagel would have been better, maybe.

"How do you know Zip?" Ellis asked after she swallowed her bite of food.

Talia washed down the scone with some coffee. She wondered if Ellis would go back to Zip and tell him everything. But this wasn't her family.

"Um, I don't really know him. He was at the bar that night and pulled the guy off me."

Ellis put her coffee down and reached across the table to squeeze her hand. "I'm sorry that happened to you. At least Zip was there. Are you pressing charges?"

Talia couldn't help but laugh. "No. Sorry, but that's just part of going to see my sister."

Ellis froze. "What?"

"My family is messed up. They don't like me."

"Not liking family is one thing, but sending someone to beat you up, that's unconscionable."

Talia stared at Ellis for a moment. "You think so?"

Ellis nodded. "Yes. That's totally wrong. Do you want to press charges?"

Talia shook her head. "No. The last time I tried to do something like that, I ended up charged with assault."

"Wait, what?"

"Yeah. They dropped the charges, but I spent four months in jail because of my family."

Ellis gasped, then shook her head. "I'm sorry. That's awful. How did you cope?"

Talia shrugged. "It's not the worst thing they've done to me. It sucked, but it was better than being at home." She couldn't tell Ellis what else her family had forced her into. Few people could reconcile what she'd done. She'd lost friends once they found out, and she didn't want to lose Ellis. "After that, I got my own place. It's not much, but I couldn't live with my family. Now I live in that apartment above the restaurant. It's only one room, but it's mine, and I don't have to worry about them coming into my room while I sleep."

Ellis looked disgusted, no, shocked. Talia hadn't even told her the bad stuff. No question, she had to keep a lid on all the other stuff that happened.

Ellis squeezed her hand again. "You're strong. No wonder Zip likes you."

"What?" She sat up and leaned forward. Ellis's words were shocking. She'd thought for sure Zip wouldn't be interested. "How do you know he likes me?"

Ellis's lips quirked up. "He asked me to give you his number."

"Oh." She'd wondered how she would get his number, and she hadn't needed to worry. Zip wanted her to have it.

"He's a good guy."

Talia nodded. "He seems like it. How long have you known him?"

"Since I started dating Trip. Some of the guys are rough around the edges, but once you get to know them, you see they are good."

She wouldn't reveal her theory that Zip was a cinnamon roll. He would probably be embarrassed and she didn't want to do that. At least not behind his back. If his cheeks went red, she wanted to see.

A woman with red hair came over to the table and Ellis jumped up, giving her a hug. "Ginger, this is Talia. Ginger has been one of my best friends for years."

Ginger didn't blink or make a face when she turned to Talia. Either these women knew to expect the cuts and bruises, or they were great actors. The woman smiled and shook her hand, acting like her sitting in this coffee shop with her messed up face was normal. "Talia, it's nice to meet you. I hope Ellis brings you around for girls' night out." Ginger's phone buzzed and she rolled her eyes. "Sorry, Kent and the child are waiting for me in the car."

Ellis pulled Ginger close for another hug before stepping back. "I'll talk to you later. Bye."

"She seems nice," Talia said as Ellis took her seat.

Ellis chuckled. "Don't let her fool you, she's a snarky bitch when we're alone but I love her."

Wistfulness filled Talia and she might have even sighed. "That's good."

Ellis leaned in. "I don't want to overstep any boundaries, but if you're good with it, would you like to come to dinner on Friday?"

"Oh, I'm working Friday evening."

"How about on Saturday?"

Talia nodded. "Yes. That would be good."

"Awesome. You can meet Trip, and we can get to know each other better. I have a feeling we're going to be friends."

Talia smiled, but inside, her stomach clenched. What would this woman say if she knew the truth of her past? Most women didn't want her near their men once they learned about her past sex work. She'd been thirteen when her sister forced her into the business. Her work paid their bills back then. She'd brought in all the money for food and the mortgage. She'd also sent her family on fabulous trips while she was literally working her ass off.

6

Zip finished his shower and was pulling on his pants when Trip stepped into the room. The look in Trip's eyes made him pause. "What?"

"You don't have to do this, but Ellis invited Talia over for dinner on Saturday."

A part of Zip wanted to tell Trip no way, but another part wanted to find out if they could make it sooner. She hadn't called, although Ellis had given her his number. Maybe she wasn't interested.

"Like I said, you don't—"

"I'll be there."

Trip slowly nodded. "Only if you're sure."

"I can't get her out of my mind. Maybe seeing her will allow me to forget her."

Trip chuckled. "Once they get under your skin, it's impossible to get them out of your mind."

He shook his head. Hopefully, he would be able to see her and forget about her. He had three days until dinner with her, and he wasn't sure he could wait that long. That night, he had to jack off before sleep would come. She was doing a number on him, and he liked it. When he found hookups, he never thought of them after sex ended. There might have been one or two women he wouldn't have minded seeing again, but only to fuck, nothing more. With Talia, he wanted to get to know her and find out what made her tick. He wanted to see if they connected.

The next few days seemed to drag by. On Saturday, he was so amped up he had to go for a second run and jack off in the shower before heading to Trip's house. He got there early and was sad that Talia wasn't already there.

"Hey," Trip said as he opened the door.

The house smelled like an Italian restaurant. Ellis had upped their food game. She and Vera went to great lengths to improve the quality of what they ate when they got together. They still had hotdogs and hamburgers at the park, but when they got together at someone's house, she and Vera made excellent food that they all appreciated.

"It smells terrific."

"Thank you," Ellis said as she came over to give him a hug.

"It's good to see you."

Ellis stepped back and nodded. "Same. How are you doing?"

"Good. How about you?"

Ellis chuckled. "Excellent. Trip is keeping me on my toes."

"Don't let her fool you, she's the one keeping me on my toes." Trip shook his hand and then leaned in and kissed Ellis's cheek. Zip turned away, not liking the jealousy sliding along his spine. He was happy for Trip and Hop. They'd found women who were awesome, who didn't back down from a challenge. He'd seen firsthand that Vera and Ellis had made his buddies better people. They were more relaxed when they weren't grinding and yet also more focused on missions.

He heard a car outside, and his heart sped up. He turned to the door, wondering if he should step outside to greet her.

Ellis moved to the window, pulling back the curtain. "It's her."

Without even thinking, Zip moved to the door and pulled it open, his stomach tightening as she stepped from the car. Her lips spread into a wide smile as she moved to him.

"Hello, Zip."

"Hello." His voice sounded strained, and he hated that.

She chuckled and moved in close, giving him a quick hug. Her lips were at his ear. "It's good to see you, Cinnamon Roll."

Her breath on his neck made his dick twitch. She was going to push him to the edge of reason without even trying. He had to prove to her he wasn't a cinnamon roll. If they got involved, she would be disappointed.

"Hey, Talia. Get in here," Ellis called out from behind him.

He wished they were alone. He should have gone to her place and waited for her to get home. He could have stalked her and showed her that he wasn't a good person. She would send him away because he wasn't worth the trouble. Instead, he had to deal with eating dinner in front of his friends while sitting across from her. Trip would call him out for being a jerk if he acted like he knew he should so she would run fast away from him. The more time he spent with her, the harder it would be to leave. Even now, just a few minutes in, he was already thinking of ways to get her to see him again.

Talia getting close would wreck him. Already, he wanted her breath on his neck again. Having her close had stirred thick desire inside. She would fit perfectly underneath his body. But he felt this was more than just the sex. She would fit perfectly in his life. Now, he just had to get to know her better.

Talia almost threw up on the way over. This man had the ability to totally wreck her. Just being close to him set her on fire. It had been a long time since she'd felt this way about anyone. After the years she'd spent working in the sex industry, few guys turned her on. It was like her libido dried up more each time she had to have sex. How she'd put up with it for the years she had was a mystery to her.

The scent of the food hit her as she stepped into the house. "Wow, it smells terrific. What did you make?" she asked as she hugged Ellis.

"Lasagna and garlic bread. I have a salad we

can eat now. The rest of the food should be ready to eat in about twenty minutes."

"Well it smells great and I'm very hungry. Thank you for cooking for us. I brought cookies. I didn't bake them, or we'd all get sick. Just so you know, they're safe."

"Thank you." Ellis turned to her man. "This is Trip."

Trip stuck out his hand for her to shake. "It's nice to meet you, Talia. Thank you for coming to dinner. Ellis has been looking forward to this all week."

She might have gasped as shock hit. Few people were ever happy to see her. She worked hard, and people at work were usually glad she showed up, but few people wanted to hang out with her.

On the plus side, neither of the men recognized her from the videos she'd been in. At least that was a good thing. She would have to tell Zip, or she could walk away and never look back. That would be the smart option, but it wasn't what she wanted. Eventually, one of his friends would recognize her, and then it would get weird.

Back when she was a teenager, she hadn't really known better. Her sister had forced her to work, but she'd enjoyed the attention. It had only been really odd when they'd forced her to work with old men. Having some grandpa doing things to her body had been disturbing.

She pushed thoughts of her past from her mind and focused on Zip. For now, until he found out the truth, she would enjoy whatever they had. Once he learned what she'd done in her past, he would dump her soon enough.

The guys served the salad while she and Ellis sat. It was the first time a guy had prepared food for her while telling her to sit down. She enjoyed listening to the men talk but had little to add to the conversation.

A timer rang, and Ellis hopped up. "Sit down, love," Trip said. "I've got it." He turned to Talia and lifted his eyebrows. "Are you really hungry, or just average hungry?"

"I'll take a smaller portion for now."

"Sure. You can always go back for seconds."

Zip got up and took her bowl. She shook her head and met his gaze when he turned after putting their dishes in the sink. She hadn't meant to say anything but couldn't hold back. "This is weird. Why are you two doing this?"

"What?" Zip asked.

"Waiting on us."

Zip shrugged. "Ellis spent the afternoon cooking, and you're a guest."

"But so are you."

Trip moved to stand beside Zip, draping his arm over Zip's shoulder. "Some people think it's weird. Lord knows I know enough Navy men who think it's the wife's job to serve him, but we serve each other. If I cook, she helps clean, and it goes the other way. Zip is just a good guy who values people."

She nodded. "It makes sense, but honestly, I've never once had any guy help me like you two are helping. So it's not an act?"

Ellis laughed as she shook her head. "No, not an act. They do this. Hop, too. He's with Vera."

She shook her head. "I'm surprised. It's not what I grew up with."

Trip was back with a plate for her. "So, what did you grow up with?"

Her throat went dry, and she had to look down at the table. She stabbed the lasagna with her fork, wondering exactly how much to tell them. They wouldn't understand.

"You don't have to tell us," Ellis said.

She looked up, seeing three pairs of eyes staring at her. Pressure increased in her ears, and the roar started. She dragged in a ragged breath, trying to keep from passing out. The world swam before her. It was a protection mechanism she'd developed over the years. Passing out changed situations and oftentimes saved her from more humiliation. But these people weren't here to abuse her. They were just curious.

"It's okay. Zip already knows my sister is awful. They did…things. I've worked hard to get away. I shouldn't have gone to the bar." She couldn't tell them that her work had paid for that bar. It would only raise questions that she didn't want to answer.

"Why did you go?" Zip's voice was quiet and held no accusations.

She turned, swallowing at the lump in her throat from the concern in his eyes. "I heard someone putting a hit on the place. I tried to warn my sister, but she's a terrible person and wouldn't let me talk. She threatened to send someone after me in the parking lot, and I hid in the bathroom until I could get a car to come pick me up. Stupid move, I know."

"Not stupid," Ellis said. "You were trying to stay safe."

"It didn't work. Her goon found me." She

waved her hand at her face, where the bruises had faded to yellow with some green still left.

"I'm glad I was able to stop him."

Talia nodded. "Yeah, thank you. No one else would have ever helped me."

Zip shook his head. An intensity filled his eyes that almost scared her. "If I'd known it was that bad for you, I would have done damage that jerk wouldn't forget."

His words made her gasp. No one had ever stood up for her. Any progress she made, she had to fight and scrap for it.

"I'm glad Zip found you," Trip said.

Her gaze shot to him. "Why?"

"Because you seem like a nice person. And Ellis likes you. That's enough for me."

She shook her head as heat rose. There was no way she could tell them what she'd done, but she had to warn them. "I'm not that good of a person."

Elis reached across the table and took her hand. "Don't let what other people said or did to you define you. You get to define yourself."

The words hit hard, bringing tears to her eyes. She didn't want to cry, but these people were being nice to her. No one had been nice in ages. To her horror, more tears slid down her cheeks. She couldn't be in here. She stood, racing to the bathroom she'd spied earlier.

Zip's strong arms caught her before she could make it to the door. He pulled her close, and she buried her face against his chest. Embarrassment and anger rose, but his arms around her made everything better.

"It's okay, Talia. I'm here for you."

His soft voice, along with his strong arms, brought more tears. She couldn't believe this man wasn't making fun of her or trying to force her to do something sexual. He was holding her like he cared. She should have pushed him away and walked, but she didn't. Her fingers twisted tighter in his shirt, and she pulled him closer.

After a few minutes, he walked them into the bathroom and got a cloth wet before gently wiping her cheeks. She stared into his brown eyes, wondering what he was thinking.

She was about to say something when his gaze met hers. No question, this guy was all gooey cinnamon roll. But did she deserve a cinnamon roll? He didn't give her a chance to think as he bent, stopping when their lips were almost touching. Five seconds ticked past, with neither of them moving.

Then she squeezed his side, and that must have been what he'd been waiting for.

When his lips came down on hers, they both moaned. The heat between them sizzled. They were molten and could easily get in trouble. She had to tell him. That thought cooled her off fast, and she ended the kiss and stepped back.

"We shouldn't. You shouldn't. It will be dangerous for you."

He cupped her cheek. "I don't care what we should or shouldn't do. And I love danger. Come to my place after this. Not for sex. We won't do that yet, but I want to spend more time with you."

She stepped back, crossed her arms over her chest and squeezed her upper arms, trying to hide her body and make herself smaller.

"Spend more time? Is that code for fucking me?"

He shook his head. "No, it's not. I won't lie. I want you. But for some strange reason, I really want you. Not for one night, either."

She shook her head, unable to believe him. "You don't want me. I'm damaged goods. There's nothing."

He cupped her cheeks and leaned in so she had

to look into his eyes. "Don't discount yourself. You're not damaged goods."

"You don't know what I've done."

"I don't care. Nothing can damage you. Not like that. You're a good person, and I want you to remember that."

Anger rose. "You don't know."

His lips thinned, and she could tell he wasn't giving up. "No, I don't. And it doesn't matter. You don't know what I've done."

She scoffed. "There's no way you've done anything as bad as I've done. I fucked up."

"Babe, we all have stuff in our pasts, but you aren't damaged."

His blind faith in her added to his words was too much. She shook her head violently, trying to get him to realize he was wrong.

"You don't know. I've done things that are unforgivable. I'm a terrible—" She couldn't tell him, not now. She couldn't stand to see the disgust on his face. She had to get out of there. It was too much.

She ran, glad she had her keys in her pocket. As she raced out the door, she yelled thank you, unsure if Ellis heard. She couldn't deal with Zip thinking she was a good person without knowing the whole story. Telling him everything was too difficult. It was better to walk away before things got good between them.

7

Zip watched her drive away, trying to decide if he should go after her or go home. She was fighting against the getting to know him stage. Why? She seemed interested, but when things got bad, she froze him out.

"What are you going to do?" Trip asked.

Zip huffed out a breath. "I don't know."

"Sure you do. You're going after her. I can see it on your face."

"Am I that obvious?"

Trip nodded. "Yep. Go find out what's bugging her. It sounds like she's had a hard life."

Zip let go of a heavy sigh. He could walk away. There would be no harm. But he would never forgive himself.

The idea of never seeing her again wasn't pleasant. They may not end up together, but he wanted a chance.

He pulled in front of the restaurant and spied her car parked down the block. She was home. His palms were damp as his nerves increased. Being this nervous hadn't happened in a long time. Even going in on a mission didn't feel like this. The stakes were higher with Talia. He realized she had the ability to crush him.

He didn't want to lose her. Not yet. Maybe this would be the end. They'd go their separate ways and never see each other again. That would be okay. No, it wouldn't. He didn't want this to be over.

* * *

TALIA WAS SO EMBARRASSED. Having Zip that close, the intensity in his eyes burning through her had been too much. Leaving had felt like the only answer.

Shame filled her as she headed inside. Her past was littered with bad decisions. Some of those decisions hadn't been hers, but they still haunted her.

She moved to the refrigerator and pulled out a

bottle of wine. She cracked it open and poured a hefty glass. The first sip was on her tongue when a knock sounded at her door. Ignoring the intruder was a possibility, but she didn't want her landlord complaining about noise. He'd been absent for a few days, but that didn't mean he didn't have people keeping account of her mistakes.

There was no peephole or a window to look and see who it was. She just had to be prepared to defend herself once the door was open.

She yanked, ready to push the person down the stairs if necessary. The sight of Zip shocked her, and she froze.

"We should talk." Zip stepped into her place, and she thought about telling him no, but he was right. They needed to talk so she could end this. There was no way he would want her after he learned the truth.

"Fine. Do you want wine?"

"No. And why are you mad at me?"

She took a long draw on the wine and then met his gaze. "I'm not mad at you. I'm pissed because my life is so fucked up, and there's nothing I can do about it."

"How fucked up could it be?"

Anger was like acid in her belly. Before, she'd

wanted to hide the information from him. Now, she wanted him to know. She wanted him to understand why he should never come around again.

She took another long drink and met his gaze, frowning as the words started assembling in her mind. "I'm trash."

"No, you're—"

"Shut up and listen." She drank the last of the glass, anger boiling over. "When I was thirteen, my sister forced me into doing videos. She whored me out on the weekends. Eventually, one of your friends is going to recognize me."

Zip's intense expression could cut glass. She didn't step back, though she could feel the heat coming off him. It was like watching an explosion without the actual explosion.

"Your sister? The woman at the bar?"

His eye twitched, and his lips thinned. She glanced down, noticing that his fists were clenched. She took a step back, and he relaxed visibly before he closed the distance between them. His hands cupped her face and the look in his eyes made her shiver.

"You were a child. You didn't do that."

"Your friends won't know that."

"If someone has a problem with you, first off,

I'm going to ask them why they are watching videos with kids in them, and secondly, I'll tell them to shut the fuck up."

She blinked up at him, studying his face for any deception. "I was fucked by a lot of guys. I don't know the body count because it was so many dudes."

"I don't give a shit if you fucked ten thousand men back then. You were a child, and they forced you to do it."

"She did force me. When I hit twenty, they stopped forcing me because I was too old."

"Not one bit of it bothers me—the number of men you had sex with. It bothers the hell out of me that your sister did that to you. If I see her again, I can't promise what I'll do." His body shook, and she froze, hoping he wasn't about to blow up. "Why did you go there to warn her about someone coming after her?"

She shrugged. "I've tried to break away, but history and stuff. I don't know. I feel like I have to do something."

"No. Never again. I don't want to tell you what to do, but your sister should never be in your life. You need to totally cut her out. We're your family now. Those people from your past don't matter."

She took a step back and held up her hand. "People could recognize me. Are you sure you're okay with guys saying things? It can get gross when I meet people out in the wild."

"I dare them to say anything to you. You're under my protection now."

"What does that mean?"

He huffed out a breath. "It means they have to go through me."

She narrowed her gaze. "Why are you doing this?"

"Because, for some reason, you've crawled under my skin."

"You're acting like a cinnamon roll."

His lips thinned, and she couldn't stop the laughter from bubbling up. His expression softened, and she reached out, placing her hand on his chest.

"Thank you."

He shrugged. "I'm just doing what anyone else would do."

She shook her head almost violently. "Heck no. No one else would care. When people find out I did porn, they leave. And my sister always makes sure my friends know what happened."

"I don't care about that. It doesn't define you."

"I want you to remember that when your

friends figure out that I was in some video they watched at some point in the past. What are you going to do then?"

"Not going to be soft on them. I'll tell them to shut it or else."

Honestly, she didn't believe him. When guys started ragging him about it, he would fold. She knew from history that's what guys did. For now, she would humor him but never get attached. Getting close only brought heartache, and she could feel it in her bones that she was one heartache away from a total breakdown.

8

Zip hated what he'd learned about Talia. Not that she'd done porn. That didn't matter to him. He'd killed people, so who was he to judge? It was funny to him that he'd gone from trying to prove to her he wasn't a good person to bending over backward to get her to trust him.

He'd wanted to stay and end up in bed with her, but he'd left, making sure she locked up behind him. He texted first thing in the morning, wanting her to know he was thinking of her.

When she responded, he decided he wanted to see her. He called, hoping she picked up.

"Hey, what's up?" Talia's voice sounded like she'd just woken. His stomach tightened as desire rose.

"I was wondering if you wanted to go for a walk on the beach?"

He could hear her yawning on the other end of the line. "Give me a few minutes to wake up."

"Sure. I'll be there in twenty minutes."

"Gosh, you're chipper in the morning. I bet it's because of the Navy. They make you get up early and shit, right?"

"Sometimes they don't even let us go to bed. I've got to say that living off base is nice. It's quieter, that's for sure."

"I'll try to be awake enough to talk, but I'm not one for the morning."

"I'll remember that. I'll see you in a few."

He was glad she wanted to hang out. He really wanted to get to know her. He pulled on his socks, worry striking hard. What was he doing? He'd gone from never wanting a relationship to tracking down a woman he hadn't even had sex with to spend the morning with her. He must be out of his mind.

TALIA FINISHED DRESSING and stepped into the bathroom. She picked up her lipstick and held it up. Why was she even trying? No question, this guy would leave once he figured out exactly what her being in porn meant. A part of her wanted to run into someone who remembered her time on screen and show Zip exactly how awful it could be.

She heard a car door shut outside and figured it was Zip. Few people showed up this early on Sunday for the restaurant, and no one else should be looking for her.

The knock on her door made her heart rate pick up. She hoped it was Zip and not someone else. There was a small probability her sister would show up, but she doubted Cheryl would stop by. They usually left each other alone, except for when she thought warning her sister about danger was a good idea.

She opened the door, relieved to see Zip. "Ah, it is you."

"If you're going to stay living here, you need to have a peephole. I'll put it in this afternoon."

"The landlord—"

"They can shut up. It's California. They have to provide one for you, but they haven't. I'll put it in so you can see who is at your door."

She stared at him, shocked that he cared. No one had ever cared this much about her.

"You okay with that?" His question seemed ridiculous after telling her what he was going to do.

She shrugged. "Yes. Thank you. I'm surprised."

"Don't be. How about we stop by a bagel place I know and grab some coffee and something to eat? Then we can head out to the beach."

"Sure. Sounds good. It has been ages since I've been at the beach before noon."

"I like it better. Fewer people. Lots more space to have conversations without someone encroaching."

She nodded and stepped outside. He took her key and locked up for her, testing the door before he stepped away. They were on the way in minutes and the stop to get bagels didn't take long.

When they stepped out of the car at the beach, he led her over to one of the park benches. It was nearly magical being here with him, the low light bouncing off the waves, a few people jogging, and one family about fifty yards away with kids playing in the sand. It wasn't anywhere near as crazy as the crowds were when she usually showed up.

They munched on their food, sitting quietly. She enjoyed his company. It was nice that neither of them felt any need to talk.

She turned to him, wondering if this was what

being together with someone was supposed to feel like.

"I guess you like the food and coffee."

She nodded. "Yes. It's good. I've never been there before. I usually work late and don't go out in the morning."

"You know I'm in the Navy. What do you do?"

She shrugged. "Nothing impressive."

"Why don't you tell me, and I'll decide for myself."

"Jesus, you're annoying."

His shoulders shook as he laughed. She liked the way his lips spread in a smile, too. "Yeah. I'm annoying. So spill. What do you do for work?"

"I clean buildings three nights a week. Then I deliver food the other days. Sometimes I work late, sometimes early. It just depends."

"So, cleaning buildings, you mean inside or outside?"

"Inside. Like picking up trash, cleaning the bathrooms, and vacuuming, though a lot of companies are using robot vacuums, so we don't have to spend hours moving the vacuum."

"That's impressive. Do you know how filthy places would be if you didn't do that? When I was in boot camp, we learned why cleaning was necessary. Let me tell you, people are disgusting."

"Oh, I know."

"So yeah, your job is impressive."

She didn't know what to say about his reaction. He'd surprised her when he didn't care that she'd done porn, and now he was impressed that she was a cleaner. He wasn't at all what she expected.

"What do you do with the Navy? Most Navy guys have short hair and none of this stuff." Talia patted the fuzz on his cheek.

He shrugged. "I'm not regular Navy."

She narrowed her gaze as confusion swirled. "Oh. What does that mean?"

His lips thinned and his eyebrows rose. "You don't know?"

She shook her head. "I never paid attention. A lot of the guys in those videos were military. I've never really had a good impression of military types."

His lips curled and he looked disgusted. For a second she thought he was angry at her, but then he shook his head.

"I'm not like them. I'm special forces. I don't fuck around with regulations. I follow the rules and keep my nose clean. Not saying I'm perfect, but losing my job would more than suck and doing shit like what they did to you would break rules that would get me kicked out."

She was surprised by his words. She'd never even considered that the men could get in trouble for what they'd done. "You seem like a rule follower."

"Really? You see that?"

"Yeah. You seem like a good person."

He shrugged. "As long as you're on my good side, I am."

She finished her bagel and noticed he was done, too. "Want to walk?"

"Sure. I'd like that."

They headed toward the water, and midway there, he took her hand. Her hand in his felt good. She was having intense feelings for him, and it scared her. She would pull back. She had to. But not yet. Zip made her feel special and she wanted to spend more time with him. Surely it wouldn't hurt for her to spend a few weeks getting to know him, enjoying his company, maybe fooling around a bit.

They were on their way back to the car when she noticed a guy looking at her weirdly. Her stomach twisted. This couldn't be good. The man was older, around forty. He was about the right age for men who would have watched the porn she'd been featured in.

Zip wasn't paying attention, or it didn't seem like he was. Her stomach twisted when the guy pointed at her and started talking to his friend and then he held up his phone.

"Shit." She shouldn't have let the word slip out, but she couldn't hold back.

"What's wrong?" Zip asked.

She shook her head. "Nothing."

He glanced around and held her hand tighter. The men were coming their way. She hated that Zip had to see this. He would walk, no question. This would be the last time they went for coffee and bagels, the last time they walked on the beach together. This was it. She would never see him again.

"Hey, aren't you Natalie Goodgirl?" the guy called out.

Heat washed over her as the old name she'd performed under hit her ears. She wanted to hide. Both guys lifted their phones like they were going to take photos of her. They were close enough that she could see the color of their eyes.

Zip didn't say anything, making her feel the loss so deeply it made her heart hurt. Then he moved so fast it made her yelp. He had their phones and was doing something. As he punched things on their screen, he started speaking.

"Let me teach you a lesson right now. Don't you ever talk to another woman like that again. Better, don't speak to women again. I'm deleting your videos and photos—"

"You can't do that!" one of the guys yelled.

"Really? Because I just did. Erased it from your system completely. I don't know who you think my girlfriend is, but I'm here to tell you, it doesn't matter. You aren't even going to look at her again. You feel me?"

Both men dropped their heads and stared at the ground. They weren't smiling or laughing any more. They seemed scared.

Zip continued speaking as he pulled out his phone. "Now then, if you ever speak disrespectfully to another woman and I find out, I'll hunt you down. I'm connecting to your social media, and I'll watch. I can find out where you live, and I will make your life hell if you ever do anything like this again. Do you understand?"

Both men nodded. Zip handed them back their phones and then took her hand, leading her away from the mess. She glanced back, noticing the men were looking the other way. Zip had shut them down. But this wouldn't be the last time something like this happened. Could he keep it up?

They were at his car, and he opened the door. She slid in and waited for him to walk around and get in. Would he tell her goodbye after this?

When he slid into the driver's seat she spoke, still looking straight ahead. "You know that won't be the last time something like that happens."

He put his hand on the steering wheel and blew out a heavy sigh. He turned his head and stared at her. "Then I'll do the same thing again."

"You can't stop all the men from being jerks."

"No, but I can stop some by standing up for you."

"I'm not having sex with you just because you did that."

He nodded. "I wouldn't expect you to. When we decide to have sex, I want you to want me, not think you owe me. If we never have sex, I'm fine with that, too. I get hard in your presence, and sure, I want you, but I would never force it."

"Why are you so good to me?"

He shook his head. "This isn't good. This is the minimum of how it should be. I'm just above average at best."

"No, no way. You're freaking amazing, and don't forget it."

"So are you, then. And don't you forget it."

She couldn't believe Zip stood up for her and he wasn't trying to fuck her. That surprised the heck out of her. She reached over and put her hand on his leg as he started the engine.

She could allow herself to feel hope, but Zip was making her wonder if good things were possible. It had been a long time since she'd felt good about her future. Maybe her luck was changing.

Zip installed the peephole and left, a little sad Talia had to go in and clean office buildings tonight. He wished they could spend the evening together, but they both had lives to work around. She wasn't working on Wednesday, so they agreed to get together and eat dinner.

That night, he thought about the two men who'd approached her. It pissed him off. A huge protective wave rose, and he wanted to keep other men away from her. But he couldn't lock her behind doors and force her to never go out in public. That would be just as bad.

Sleep wasn't his friend, and when his alarm rang, he climbed out of bed and stumbled to the coffee pot. He hoped Talia had at least gotten some sleep. He knew she had been at work until after midnight, so he didn't text even though he wanted to. He would send her something later.

They spent the morning going over reports on questionable activities in Eastern Europe. He hated that the world couldn't just calm down and get along. He knew that would never happen, but he wished people could just be decent to each other for a few years, maybe just a few months would work.

"Zip, how is Talia?" Trip asked as he walked beside him.

"She's good."

"Ellis said she was going to swing by and talk to her today."

Zip stopped, and Trip pulled up and turned to face him. He needed to get Trip to understand that he wouldn't walk away from Talia. He knew guys were weird about their girlfriends having sex with other people. Guys got downright possessive when it came to their girlfriends and wives. If they knew some other Navy guy slept with their girl, they went off. Any guys who dated sex workers were razzed, and their friends tried to break them up.

"What?" Trip asked.

"I don't know what Talia will share, but I want to make sure you understand I'm not leaving her. I know what she went through in her past, and it doesn't matter to me."

Trip sobered, and his lips turned down. "What did you find out?"

Zip blew out a breath. "It's not my place to say. If she wants to share, that's up to her. But I'll tell you this much, she's stronger than any of us. I respect her and the choices she has made."

Trip nodded as he crossed his arms over his chest. "Sounds serious."

Zip nodded. "She may be rough around the edges, but she's good."

"I trust you, Zip. You're a good man, and you've got a good head on your shoulders. If you vouch for her, I don't care what anyone else says about her."

Zip nodded. "Thank you."

"Hey, guys, you ready to eat?" Q called out.

"Sure am," Trip replied.

Zip hoped Trip would keep everything on the down low. He hated gossip and knew guys were the worst. If the wrong man found out, it would be all over the base by morning. A shiver worked through him. He wouldn't walk away from Talia, but from what he knew about people, this was going to be a bumpy ride.

Later that afternoon, his team, along with a few

other teams, headed to the obstacle course for training. Preacher and Blink were in front of him, chatting about what they thought they were training for when Kevlar came over.

"Hey, Zip. Saw you this weekend with your girl."

Zip's muscles tightened. He hoped Kevlar wasn't going to say something stupid. He didn't want to argue with other SEALs, but he sure as fuck wasn't going to let any guys disrespect Talia.

"Yeah. We were out."

"I didn't know you were dating anyone."

"Just started."

"Well, just wanted to say if you have problems with anyone, I'm here."

Zip narrowed his gaze, trying to figure out what the man meant. He didn't have to wonder for long. Kevlar leaned in, putting his hand on Zip's shoulder.

"I was on the beach. Don't worry, I have your back."

"Oh. Thanks."

Kevlar walked away and moved over to where Rider, Wild, and Sharp were standing. They were getting information from one of the lieutenants.

SEALs were a different breed. They stuck together, family and all that.

He didn't have time to think as they started the exercise. They stayed late and by the time he got home, exhaustion ruled. He ate leftovers and headed to bed after sending Talia a text. She'd sent one earlier, but he knew she was working and it would be after midnight before she was free.

He couldn't wait until Wednesday when he got to see her again. He wasn't sure how much Kevlar had seen or heard on the beach, but he hoped Kevlar wasn't into gossiping. Keeping Talia's secret wouldn't be easy, but with friends like Kevlar having his back, he wasn't as worried as he had been before.

10

Talia delivered groceries on Wednesday and was on her last delivery. She was excited to see Zip. They'd texted a few times, talking about nothing much, just sharing things like what kind of food they liked and which restaurants they avoided.

She pulled up at the address and grabbed the bags. She was halfway to the door when it opened, and a middle-aged man stepped out. She hated when men stepped out as she was carrying up a bunch of bags.

"You can come on in and set it on the counter."

"No, sir. I can not. I'll leave them here for you."

"No, that won't do. I need you to bring them inside."

"I'm not going inside your house."

"Come on, you know you want it."

Anger filled her. She hated being treated less than human. She put the bags down, bending at the knees as she kept her eyes on the guy. There was no trusting a guy like him.

Before she could stand, he lunged, and she jerked back, landing on her ass. The man started laughing as she scrambled up and took off toward her car. Her hands shook, and her heart raced as she took off. She was never happier that she had a car with a push-button start than at that moment. If she'd had to fuss with keys, she would have been sitting there long enough for that bastard to attack.

A few blocks away, she pulled into a parking lot and marked the address as somewhere she would never deliver again. After detailing the interaction, she blew out a breath, wishing life wasn't so shitty. Maybe she did bring it on herself like her sister said she did.

Once home, she showered, noticing her lower back and rear were sore from falling. Anger rose, and she was thinking of some way to go back and make that man pay when her phone buzzed. Zip had texted, stating that he was ready for her to come over. He wanted to make her dinner. She shrugged, thinking it sounded good. She texted back that she would be there in about twenty minutes.

Dating someone who knew about what happened to her was weird. She was glad it seemed like he didn't care, but eventually it would become something for him, and he would leave just like all the other people in her life had.

By the time she made it to Zip's place, she'd calmed down some. She no longer wanted to randomly kill people who got in her way. Getting this angry wasn't healthy, but she didn't have money for therapy.

Zip opened the door as she was on her way up to his door and stood with open arms. The pressure and pain of the day hit hard, and she moved to him, wrapping her arms around his waist. He hugged her back, holding her tight before he stepped them inside and closed the door.

"How was your day?" Zip asked when they were inside.

"Fuck." She hadn't wanted to say anything but having him welcome her with open arms had broken something inside.

He leaned back and met her gaze. "What happened?"

She blew out a breath and shook her head. "It probably wasn't anything, but my last delivery was some jerk. He came outside and met me on his porch, telling me I had to go inside his house to set the bags down on his counter."

"What the hell?"

"Yeah. I set the bags on the ground. He lunged toward me while I was placing them, and I fell. My ass hurts."

Zip chuckled. "I'm not going to offer to kiss it."

His words made her laugh. It felt good to laugh about it. She'd been so hot before, but now that she was in Zip's arms, she could see the funny side.

Zip stopped laughing and sobered. "I want you to be careful while you're out there. Do you have mace?"

She shook her head. "No. I used to, but it was cheap, and the thing broke. Ruined my purse."

"I'll buy you some that is good. I want you to practice using it."

"How?"

"We could use a spray bottle. You don't have to mace me, though I have been maced before. It's part of our training so you could if you feel you need to."

She nodded. "I wouldn't want to mace you. I guess we could practice with a spray bottle."

"I want you to feel safe."

"I wish I didn't have to work two jobs, but I can't make it without the extra money delivering stuff."

"I'm sorry that happened to you."

She nodded. "Yeah. How was your day?"

He shrugged. She wondered if he was going to stay silent when he turned to face her, his lips down in a frown. Worry hit.

"What?"

"One of the other SEALs was at the beach. He saw me confront those two jerks."

Heat filled her, racing up her neck to her face. Breathing became difficult, and her head started to swim. Zip held onto her elbows and lowered his head, locking his gaze with hers.

"He said he had my back. I don't know how much he heard, but he told me he supports me— us."

She shook her head. "He doesn't know me."

"No, but he knows me, and he knows I'm solid."

She shook her head and tried to turn. "I shouldn't—"

"No. I'm not losing you because of some idiot."

"I'm not yours."

"You may not be yet, but I'm not giving up."

Her heart swelled at his words, and her throat closed. He knew what to say to make her feel like she couldn't walk away from him. She hated that she was becoming dependent on him. He could easily crush her, but she couldn't pull away, not yet. She wanted to see what was next for them.

11

Zip could feel the agitation and worry coming off Talia. He had to admit he would be worried, too. She'd had a rough life, been abused, and treated like shit. It would be easy to form such a hard shell no one could get in. He hoped she let him in.

He grilled steaks and vegetables and heated up mac and cheese while the steaks were on the grill. She tried to help, but he told her to sit and let him take care of everything.

When they sat to eat, the joy on her face was payment enough. After a few bites, her smile came easier.

"What do you want to do this weekend?"

Her eyebrows rose as she cut him a glance

before turning back to her food. "Your friends potentially knowing about me hasn't scared you off and you still want to see me."

"Of course, I want to see you. I enjoy spending time with you."

She took another bite, chewing thoughtfully. "I don't have a lot of money, so whatever we do, it needs to be cheap."

"How about a hike and then a picnic?"

"That sounds like fun."

He didn't want to bring up what had happened to her while working, but he did wonder if she wanted to do something else. People who had few choices in life usually didn't have time to think about the future. Maybe she was happy with her job. He needed to get to know her better.

She insisted on helping him clean up the kitchen after they finished eating. He welcomed her help, enjoying spending time with her.

After drying his hands, Zip turned to face Talia. "Do you want to watch something on TV?"

"Funny enough, I don't have a TV, so I haven't watched anything in ages. I wouldn't even know what to pick."

"I mindlessly watch in the evenings. Sometimes,

I mute the TV while I'm reading an article and forget it's on. It's a bad habit."

"What movies have you liked recently?"

He shrugged. "A new Deadpool came out."

She raised her eyebrows and shook her head. "Deadpool?"

"I take it you never saw the first one."

"Nope. Never heard of it."

"Would you like to start it?" He checked the time and shrugged. "I have three hours before I have to be in bed."

"Okay. Sure."

He grabbed a beer and poured her another glass of wine. He was happy when she sat close to him. Usually, he moved fast with women, but he was enjoying the slow burn developing between them.

The anticipation brewing inside was more exciting than picking up a woman at the clubs had ever been. Maybe he really was ready for a change.

* * *

SITTING BESIDE ZIP WAS NICE. The movie started, and it wasn't at all what she was expecting. The opening scene was a little too fast, and a lot happened. She almost wanted to watch it again but didn't stop the movie since she was watching it with Zip.

When they got to the sex stuff, she felt a little uncomfortable because it made her aware of just how much she wanted to be with Zip. By the end, she realized she'd missed so much of popular culture just trying to stay alive.

The credits rolled, and she sat in stunned silence. Her life had been held together with gum and crappy hair bands. Jail, homelessness, being forced into porn, all of it had made it nearly impossible to live.

"Hey."

She jerked her head up and met Zip's confused gaze. He'd been trying to show her a good time, and now she was sitting on his couch almost in tears after watching a movie that was supposed to be fun.

"Are you okay? We shouldn't have watched that movie."

She shook her head. "No, it's not that. It's not the movie. It's…" She stood and paced the length of the room, then turned back to him, noticing he was standing now, but she hadn't heard him move.

"I'm sorry," he said.

"No." Agitation filled her. "There's nothing for

you to be sorry for. I just—it's my past. I just realized how much I've lost out on. I've spent my life just trying to survive, and I feel like I'll never get there."

He moved fast and had his arms around her. "I've got you."

This wasn't how she wanted this night to go, but the good food, the movie, and now him being so kind brought more tears. She clung to him, sobbing against his chest as he smoothed his hands over her hair.

After a moment, he moved to the couch and pulled her down on his lap. She clung to him, hating that she was falling apart but loving that he was here for her.

When her tears finally calmed, she sat up and met his gaze. "I'm sorry."

"Don't be. I'm happy to hold you and help you."

She shook her head. "I feel like something bad is coming for me. You shouldn't be close to me. It's dangerous."

He tapped his finger on her nose. "I'm dangerous as a fucking heart attack, and I give back more than I get. So there is no walking away from you. I'm here to stay."

"They do bad things. You could end up in trouble."

"Trouble? I eat trouble for breakfast."

"One time, I tried to press charges against them, and I ended up in jail for four months."

His lips thinned, and she swore the anger in his eyes could cut glass. "What do you mean?"

"They have cops, not San Diego police, but they have other officers in their pocket. They had me arrested and held. While in, they wouldn't feed me but once a day, and they wouldn't let me call anyone. I only got out because a group from the government came to tour the jail and found me."

"I'm sorry that happened to you. I promise that won't happen with me around."

"But you can't be around twenty-four-seven."

"No, but I have interesting friends who don't always operate in the bounds of what is legal."

"That sounds like my family."

"Except my friends work for good, not chaos."

"What exactly are we talking about?"

"One of my friends can track you. You can wear earrings, or we can place a tracker in your clothing. It could be in a watch or something like that. Then if you haven't been heard from at whatever time we decide, we track you. You can have an emergency button to send a distress call. Basically, we can get you security, which is usually reserved for heads of state, so you can feel safe."

"I don't know. I don't like the idea of being tracked."

"I get that. It would be for your safety and not to put limits on you."

She shook her head. "Why would you do this for me? Why do you care?"

He cupped her cheek and ran his thumb over her skin. "I don't know, but I do care about you. I care what happens. I don't know if we'll make it as a couple, but I still will care if something goes bad for you."

She blew out a breath, wondering how she'd found such a good man. She hadn't even been looking for someone to date, and now she had someone who cared about her.

"I don't understand."

"What's to understand?"

"Why are you being so nice? No one is this nice."

"People should be this nice. You deserve to be treated well."

Her throat closed, and words failed her, so she hugged him again. She wasn't used to anyone being this nice. She'd called him a cinnamon roll to razz him earlier, but it was the truth. He was a cinnamon roll. He was kind and sweet, and protective of her. She hoped he never changed because this felt so good. Having Zip in her life would be different from any relationship she'd ever had. He was different, and she liked it. Her past had a way of creeping in, but maybe this time was different.

12

Holding Talia felt good. They weren't even kissing but having her in his lap felt amazing. He was doing all he could to keep his cock from getting hard. She didn't need that, not now.

He was about to stand when she turned and straddled him, her body fitting perfectly against his.

"Talia," he whispered. "You don't—"

"I want to."

Her lips came down on his, and his eyes slid closed. He held onto her sides, then slowly wrapped his arms around her back as her arms came around his neck. She rocked her hips, and he knew he wasn't going to be able to control his dick. The heat in his chest spread out to his limbs. He wanted to get rid of his clothes just to cool off but also to feel all of her.

She pulled back, her lips twisted into a sexy smile. "How far do you want to take this?"

He groaned. "I should say we stop now, but I don't want to. I like how you feel against me."

She rocked her hips, grazing her center against his hardening cock. "I like this."

His hands tightened on her sides, and for a second, he held her still. He needed more, so he moved her, grinding her against his body. They both moaned and went back to kissing. He was so close to the edge. No way would he do this with any other woman. He would have pushed her off him and leaned her over the couch before grabbing a condom and sinking in. He didn't want to rush things with Talia, though. He needed more.

He had to stop this.

Zip ripped his lips from hers and held her so the pressure wasn't so hot against his dick.

"I want us, not just sex. We need to slow down."

She groaned but moved her leg, crawling off his body. "I agree. I don't want to, but I think it would be better if we waited."

"I want to get to know you, Talia. We've spent

some time together, but we need more time together."

"I should go home."

He thought about complaining and begging her to stay, but he needed to be strong. He needed to know Talia better, not just have sex with her at the drop of a hat. There was something brewing between them that felt different than anything he'd experienced before. He wanted that to grow and for anything to grow between them, it needed air.

The thought of having sex with her twisted through his mind, but it was too early. They could wait.

He jumped up and moved to her, placing a very sweet kiss on her lips while keeping their bodies apart. Touching her felt amazing. It was more than just the sexual touch, more than what he felt with others. Touching Talia pulled at his soul. She was salve to his sandpaper heart, giving him relief he'd never had before.

13

Talia wished they'd had sex, but it would have been too soon. She wanted more from Zip. He knew a lot about her, more than most people, and he hadn't run. He was sticking by her. She couldn't believe that he wanted to be with her after everything she'd done.

A knock sounded on her door, and she moved to it, glad Zip had installed the peephole. She looked through it, seeing a stranger.

"Who is it?"

"It's Dave from downstairs."

"Dave. There isn't a Dave."

"Sorry. My dad died. I own the place. I wanted to introduce myself."

Talia squeezed her hands into fists and weighed

her options. Her landlord could have died. She wouldn't have known. Now she had this guy standing outside her place, wanting to talk to her. It wouldn't do any harm, would it? She slowly opened the door, bracing her foot behind it so she could stop him from barging in.

"Yeah?"

"Like I said, I'm Dave. I own the place now. I'm not changing anything. I'll be the one you give rent to."

"I was paying online. Can we do that?"

"Sure. I'll give you my email address and information. Same price and stuff. I used to live here but moved to Los Angeles. I'm moving back so you'll see more of me."

She nodded and tried for a friendly smile. "I hope you enjoy living here."

He narrowed his gaze then shook his head. "Sorry. I thought I recognized you but I don't think so."

Fear coiled deep in her belly. Being recognized sucked, especially by someone who watched porn with young girls in it. Once she looked older, they didn't want her.

She shook her head. "Nope, I don't know you. Must be someone else."

He nodded and turned to leave but turned back. "Oh, stop by sometimes. I'll give you a discount."

She smiled and nodded. "Sure. Thank you." This guy needed to leave. He would eventually remember where he'd seen her, and then he would want something and take it. There would be no respect, no kindness, just ownership. She'd seen it before.

Bile burned in her belly. She wanted to escape. She had to leave San Diego and go somewhere no one would recognize her.

Dave headed down the stairs, and she stepped back, locking the door behind her. She slid down the flat surface of the door, angry and sad. She wanted a relationship with Zip but doubted she could hold on to what they had. Some guy would do something gross, and Zip would be pissed. There was no out for her. She may have aged some, but she still looked like herself. Maybe in twenty years, no one would recognize her as that girl from the gross porn they'd watched, but she couldn't guarantee it.

She would have to walk away from Zip to save him. He deserved better than her.

Zip texted Talia early on Thursday but didn't get a response until the end of his workday. Her reply seemed less enthusiastic than he expected. Maybe she was busy with work. Because of her work schedule, he wouldn't see her until Saturday. He couldn't wait to spend the day with her.

Early on Friday morning, he received a text that threatened to shatter his plans. He rolled his eyes when he saw they had to be at the base in less than an hour. He took a quick shower and dressed, grabbing a travel mug of coffee on the way out.

He wanted to know what was going on before he texted Talia to tell her he wouldn't be able to see her this weekend. Rider, Hop, and Q were already there when he arrived, and then Trip and Bud showed up about five minutes later.

They headed into one of the situation rooms and set up. "One of the other teams had to move into action last night to rescue a group of Marines. We need you all on overwatch. We need options. Let's keep our guys alive."

Zip read the situation report and saw that Kevlar's team was the one on the ground. He put on his coms and pulled up the screens he needed to watch. They only called them in for stuff like this when things were bad. Something awful must have happened for them to be watching everything on screens.

Being here on base, not where the action was happening, was frustrating. But when they had people watching over their shoulders, he knew he was in good hands because other SEALs had their back.

He watched as Safe and Preacher headed around a building. Smiley and Blink were on the other end of the compound. Trip and Bud were keeping their eyes on MacGyver and Kevlar.

Zip saw movement on the screen. "Safe, there are two tangos about twenty yards to your east."

"Got it."

He watched as Safe turned and took out the two men approaching. The Marines who'd gone down were about half a mile away from their location. It would have been better for them to drop closer to the building where they were being held, but that hadn't been possible.

Nothing happened for a few minutes, and then he saw more activity to the north and changed his coms, so he only spoke to people in the room. "This is about to get bad. A grenade launcher to the north."

"See it," Bud said.

Rider opened coms so Kevlar's team could hear. "You've got a grenade launcher being set up about a mile to the north."

"Fuck!" Kevlar said.

Zip watched the screen, hoping the guys were able to get to safety. The screen lit up in the area of the grenade launcher. He held his breath, hoping the guys were okay. Not being able to do anything was torture. The men on the ground were professionals, but they weren't magicians.

They were moving fast, getting out of the way of the grenades sent their way. He held his breath until all the guys were in the clear. Smiley and Blink took off in the direction of the launcher. At least they were taking care of the problem. It would take them a few minutes to intercept the launcher. They would just have to keep the guys informed about the next strike.

The rest of Kevlar's team was approaching the building where the Marines were being held. Once they had them free, hopefully, a few of the guys would be able to help fight their way out.

The world was becoming more dangerous, and the military was barely keeping up with the changing landscape. SEALs and other special forces groups were equipped, but only because their leaders understood the current condition and were making changes to how they trained.

His team was scheduled, along with Kevlar's team, to train a group of special forces Marines, but it wasn't enough. Regular military was getting left behind and put at risk. Fixing it was above his pay grade, so he would have to be satisfied with what they were doing.

It took Kevlar's team another two hours to rescue the Marines and get to safety. It was still early, so he grabbed a mug of coffee and headed into the room with their desks. Bud and Q were right behind him.

Q dropped into his chair and let go a heavy sigh. "Fuck, I hate being stuck here watching other teams."

"Same," Zip said.

"They got out," Rider said as he entered the room.

Everyone mumbled their agreement. Zip sipped his coffee, hoping Kevlar's team was enjoying their victory.

"We need to go for a run," Zip said after a moment.

The guys groaned, but they started changing into their PT clothes. His team was the best. He respected the other SEALs, but this group was family, and he would make sure they all came home from missions and deployments. His thoughts turned from his team to Talia. He wanted to make sure she survived, too. She deserved happiness, and he wanted to stay in her life and give it to her.

There was something special about the woman, and he wanted to experience more with her. She may be down on herself, but he wasn't. He didn't love the fact that she'd done porn, but it really wasn't a big deal for him. He cared more about what was in her heart, not what she'd done with her body. The thought of her family forcing her into porn made anger rise. He needed to control that anger and not lash out at Talia, so he pushed the thought away, and focused on things they could so on Saturday, like hiking one of the trails he knew about.

15

The office building she had to clean on Friday night was a disaster. It looked like someone had come in to rob it or something. The manager called their contact at the company and was assured that no one had broken into the building. They'd had a party and left a mess, not picking up anything. There was trash strewn everywhere.

She hated messy people who couldn't bother to pick up after themselves. Sure, their job was to clean, but they weren't supposed to have to pick up after spoiled brats who couldn't manage to toss stuff into the trash.

They worked late, and exhaustion was sucking

her under when she climbed the steps to her apartment. She was almost at the top before she looked up and saw Dave standing with a smirk on his face.

"Out late working?"

She paused, her brain not moving fast to keep up with why Dave was at her door and what his words meant. "What?"

His laughter made her want to run. She put her hand on the railing, trying to steady herself. She had nothing to protect herself. The mace was in her car. She hadn't thought she'd run into trouble getting into her apartment.

"I remembered where I saw you. You know, I could cut you a discount on rent."

His words sent ice through her veins. He'd watched the porn she'd been in and recognized her. Anger at her family rose, and she wanted to punish them and this jerk. But she was on the steps, a precarious position at best. He was bigger, and she had nothing to fight with.

She straightened her spine, anger and hate interwoven with her muscles, making them clench. "No, thank you."

His laughter grew, and he moved fast, pinning her against the railing. "I could just force you. No one would believe you, you little whore."

He leaned in and sniffed her neck, sending shivers down her spine. She couldn't let him rape her. She paused but wasn't frozen in place. She'd dealt with enough assholes to know what would come next. If she waited just a second, he'd think he had the upper hand.

When he finally started touching her breasts, she moved fast, lifting her knee and slamming it as hard as she could into his body. She was sore from being on her knees scrubbing stains off the carpets at work, and pain exploded down her leg, but she couldn't stop there.

Maybe her aim hadn't been great, but Dave recovered fast and grabbed her. She went down hard on her elbows, sending pain from her shoulders up her neck and down her back.

"You bitch!" he roared.

Talia kicked out, hitting Dave squarely in the nose. She was making him mad but wasn't doing much to save herself. He yanked at her ankle, pulling her down a step.

Her head bounced on the stairs, and she screamed as shock filled her. She needed to fight harder to get away, but his hand on her ankle was like a vice grip. She wouldn't escape.

Panic ramped up. Her hands were shaking so

hard she knew she wouldn't be able to fight. This was a losing battle. She was done for. No way she would survive his anger. Men like him were punishing. It wasn't enough to have sex. He would have to break her.

Her heart was pumping hard, and her breathing became erratic. Her vision blurred, and she couldn't get it together. She thought she might pass out. Going dark would be terrible. He would really take advantage of her if she dipped under. She had to stay alert and fight.

Dave yanked at her pants, pulling them down around her thighs. She kicked at him again and tried to scream, but she couldn't catch her breath enough to yell.

Then the most wonderful thing happened. She saw the flash of red and blue lights followed by someone running up the stairs. Dave was yanked off her. She pulled her legs up and wrapped her arms around them, trying to protect herself and become as small as possible.

"Miss, are you okay?"

A shiver rocked through her, and she mumbled something but was having trouble speaking. Another police car stopped, and two women got out. More tears came.

"Miss, can we call someone?"

She glanced up, seeing the officer standing above her. She whimpered and pulled away. The two women officers were there, and one sat on the step below her.

"Do you have your phone?"

The officer's soft question drew her in. She nodded and reached into her pocket, glad it hadn't been damaged during the fight.

"Do you have someone you want to call? Family?"

She shook her head and then thought about Zip. She opened her phone and hit his name, initiating the call. She didn't move the phone to her ear, so the officer took it when Zip answered.

"Hello. This is Officer Gorman. I'm with—what's your name, honey?"

Talia stared at the officer, trying to form words. "T-T-Talia."

"I'm with Talia. I think she needs to go to the hospital. Yes, sir, she's not unconscious, but she's not talking. The ambulance just showed up. You should meet her at the hospital."

Talia closed her eyes, a shudder ripping through her. Somehow, she was in the ambulance. She guessed Zip would meet her, or maybe he would realize she wasn't worth the trouble. This was just a small dose of what would happen, and it would happen again and again, just like it had happened before. Then he would run, and it would ruin any chance they had.

16

Zip had his clothes on and was out the door in minutes. He didn't speed on his way to the hospital, but it was close. Worry filled him as he glanced over and spied an ambulance arriving.

He hurried into the hospital, trying to keep his emotions under control as he asked to see Talia. It took almost thirty minutes for him to be called back. When he stepped into the curtained off area with her bed, the emotions were almost too much. He didn't know what happened, but he could see the sadness and fear on Talia's face. His heart squeezed and all he wanted was to protect her.

He moved to her, leaning in close. "I'm here."

Tears slipped out of her eyes. The curtain

opened behind him and he looked up to see a man in a long-sleeve shirt and tie.

"I'm Detective Huett. The man who attacked you was out on bail. I'm fairly certain the judge will revoke his bail, but maybe there is somewhere else you can stay for a while."

Zip didn't hesitate. "She can stay with me."

"And you are?"

"Lewis Hodge."

The detective met Talia's gaze. "Is that okay—you staying with him?"

She nodded. "Yes." Her voice was barely above a whisper.

"Okay. I'll get your information, sir. I just want to know where she is if that jerk gets released."

Zip nodded as he pushed his anger down, trying to keep it under control as he held Talia's hand. "I'll keep her safe."

The detective sized him up then nodded. "Good."

After the detective left, he held her hand, waiting for the paperwork to release her. She didn't say much, even when he asked her questions. He hated the dead look in her eyes. She was funny and snarky, but all that pep was gone. He wanted it back but forcing her to be happy wasn't realistic.

It took them a few hours before she was free to go. She was okay but had a mild concussion. The doctors wanted her to rest, and he would make sure she didn't have to worry about anything this weekend. They would figure out everything else later once they had time to talk.

Talia slowly opened her eyes, and then the memory hit as she saw she wasn't at her place. She'd been through too much shit, but she was safe right now. Zip had brought her to his home and had held her as she fell asleep. He hadn't asked any questions, just held her as she drifted off.

She found a new toothbrush in the bathroom, then an oversized shirt and some sweats that kind of fit. When she stepped out of the bedroom, Zip stood and moved to her. He brushed his fingers against her cheek and then pulled her into a hug. She was grateful he didn't ask questions.

After a moment, he leaned back and met her

gaze. "What about breakfast? I have stuff to make pancakes."

Comfort food sounded great. It was the kind of thing she'd always wanted someone to do for her but never had experienced. "That would be nice."

"Good. Why don't you sit, and I'll get everything together."

"You don't—"

"You have a concussion. The doctor wants you to rest. I'll take care of the food."

She wasn't used to having someone take care of her. It was nice, much better than fending for herself. Before this, she'd never relaxed with a guy, but with Zip, it was easy to trust him. "I guess we're not going on a hike."

He shook his head. "We can watch a movie and take naps. I didn't get much sleep this week since I had to go to base early. I'll enjoy resting with you."

"Are you sure?"

"Yes. I want to cook for you. I want to take care of you."

His suggestions sounded perfect. They could spend the day hanging out here. At least that wouldn't cost her much money. She sat on the couch, wincing as pain flared. Her rear was still sore, along with her shoulders and her head. It reminded her of her past and how she would end up being sore after a long week of filming.

Zip worked efficiently in the kitchen, not having any problems. She was impressed that he didn't seem to have any issues cleaning as he went. That was also a first. Most people made messes when they cooked. It was nice seeing how Zip did things. The lack of clutter and mess was calming. Because she lived in such a small place, she had to keep her kitchen space and bathroom clean. Zip seemed like he naturally picked up after himself.

"The first batch will be done in a few minutes. I have syrup or honey."

"Honey? Who has honey on their pancakes?"

He shrugged. "Being in the military, you get to see a lot of differences in what people like. I mean, in training situations, you eat what you're given. But if they have time to pick and choose, you see the differences. Some people, not many, eat pancakes and waffles with honey. Just like some people don't think pinto beans are real beans, but others think white beans are the best."

"I like pancakes with syrup, and pinto beans are the best."

"I agree. Now that you're staying here, you get to see my weird food habits."

She chuckled. "I'll be surprised if you want to put up with me after a few days."

His expression sobered. "I want you here and I will want you here as long as you want to stay. That place you were living, it's not safe. You don't have to move in, but I don't think you should live there."

She pulled off a piece of pancake and popped it in her mouth. It tasted great. "Did you add cinnamon?"

"Sure did. It's a trick I learned from one of the wives. She has kids, and I was over there one day helping them replace their shingles."

"You know how to shingle a house?"

He shrugged. "Not really. But I can follow directions really well. We did a great job with it. We all kind of help each other out when we can. I don't know that we'll ever shingle another house. It was hard work, but they needed an emergency repair, and we jumped in."

"Wow. I'm impressed. I've never had people who cared enough to do anything for me. I can't imagine replacing shingles on a roof."

"Well, we've got a good crew for the most part. I mean, there are some guys who are assholes, but they are few and far between."

She finished her first pancake and Zip put another one on her plate. "I probably shouldn't."

"You should if you're hungry."

She eyed the pancake and picked it up, dipping a corner into the syrup she'd poured onto her plate. Being with Zip felt comfortable. Anytime she'd lived with someone before, it hadn't been a good situation.

He sat down across from her and raised his eyebrows. "You're concentrating very hard."

She shrugged. "I've never really lived with someone I liked before. It's weird."

"How so?"

"Like you have no agenda. I mean, I know you want to have sex." Her gaze slid down his body, and when she glanced back up, his eyebrows were raised.

"Like what you saw?"

She rolled her eyes. "I would be stupid to think you didn't want to have sex."

He quirked up an eyebrow. "The question is, do you want to have sex?"

"Duh. Of course, I want to have sex with you. I just don't know if I can."

"We don't have to rush. We can take time and get to know each other better."

"So you can keep your hands off me?"

"I'm not a total jerk. If you're not ready, I can wait."

"I'm surprised."

"We certainly aren't doing anything while you're injured."

Laughter bubbled up. She felt lighter than she had in a while, though she'd just lived through something horrible.

"You're laughing. That's a good thing, I guess."

"You make me feel better. I don't know. I think it's just you're a nice guy."

Zip threw back his head, and laughter boomed through the room. Smiling up at him, she felt better than she had in ages.

"I have a load of other people who would fight you about that."

"You tried to convince me you were a jerk when we first met. But I'm right. You're a soft, squishy cinnamon roll." She stood and moved to him, putting her hands on his shoulders. She pushed him, and he dropped to the chair behind him. She was sore, but she straddled him, wrapping her arms loosely around his shoulders. "You're sweet, and I bet if I licked up your body, it would taste like sugar."

His expression changed to serious, and his eyes grew darker. "You're pushing your luck."

"I know, behave. But what if I wanted to be bad? We could be bad together."

"Jesus, woman. You're still black and blue. We're going to take this slow and just hang out. Later, after you're better, we'll test out your theory that I'm a cinnamon roll. For now, we'll hang out."

She slumped against him, resting her head on his shoulder. "Thank you for being so nice. Thank you for giving me a place to sleep where I feel safe."

"Of course. I wouldn't want you anywhere else."

She had to get off his lap, but him holding her this close felt nice. It was unfair, and she knew it. He wouldn't have sex with her until she healed and she was pressed up against him, using him like a bed.

Though she didn't want to, she pushed off his chest and stood. They both ignored his raging hard-on as she moved to the kitchen to grab more coffee and then started cleaning the space.

"Hey, you don't have to clean."

"Sorry, habit. I'm probably overly obsessive about the kitchen. Just had food poisoning too many times as a kid. I don't even like letting coffee sit in the pot. It's weird. Not the weirdest thing about me, but at least you know the kitchen will be clean."

He moved to her and kissed her on the side of her head, giving her a loose hug before stepping back. "I like a clean kitchen, too. I just don't want you wearing yourself out. I'll clean. You go sit."

She stared up at him, wondering if he would always be this nice. He wasn't like anyone else she'd ever met. Living in the same space as Zip would be challenging, but at least she felt safe. Better safe than sorry. But would he be sorry he'd let her in? She had a history that could derail them, and that fact was painfully obvious after what had happened with her new landlord. Leaving the area would be best, but she wasn't ready to walk away from Zip. Not yet.

18

Having Talia in his space was heaven and hell. She was everything he wanted, and yet he couldn't have her. Not until she healed. Even then, he knew he would be bad for her. Guys who watched porn would come onto base and assume things about her, just like her idiot landlord had.

She needed his protection, but having her close would open her up to comments that were totally unacceptable. She wasn't a toy for horny guys to use. Even if she'd gone into porn on her own volition, that wouldn't give guys the right to cross her boundaries. He didn't want to bring on trouble, but he feared that staying with her was doing exactly that.

After breakfast, she lay down for a nap, and he contacted one of his buddies who was into computers. The guys on his team were better friends with Thario than he was, but he got along with the guy.

"Hey, Zip, what do I owe this pleasure?"

He stepped outside, not wanting Talia to hear him discussing her life. "I have an issue."

"What's up?"

"I'm seeing someone who has a problem."

"What kind of problem?"

He glanced around and ducked his head, lowering his voice so none of the neighbors could hear. "If you ever meet her, you can never say anything."

"This sounds serious." Thario's voice was flatter, less friendly, more business-like.

"Just promise you won't ever hold this against her."

"You have my word."

"Okay. So her family trafficked her into porn when she was a teenager. People recognize her. I don't know if there is anything that can be done, but I don't like it. She was attacked by her new landlord. He tried to rape her."

"Fucking mother fucker. Give me the details, and I'll see what I can do."

Zip blew out a breath. "Is there really anything you can do?"

"Maybe. She was a teen, right?"

"Yes. She was thirteen."

"Fuck. Let's get to work on it. I can't destroy physical copies, but I can find shit on the dark web and go nuclear on it. I can also make anonymous reports about people viewing it. It may take a few months, but I'll scrub as much of her footprint from the web as I can."

Zip breathed a sigh of relief. "Thank you. And listen, don't tell her."

"You're thinking of not telling her what you are doing?"

"I don't want her to know because I don't know how she will take it. I don't want her to think I'm ashamed of what she did because I'm not. I don't care about that. I just want her to be safe, and she can't be safe with idiots thinking they can get a piece of her because she did something when she was younger."

"I get it. I'll see what I can do."

"Thank you."

"No problem. It gives me something to do. And Zip, don't be a stranger. Frog would love to meet her."

"We'll come by, maybe next weekend."

"Awesome. I'm looking forward to it."

Zip went inside and heard Talia stirring. He hoped she hadn't heard his discussion with Thario. The last thing he wanted was for her to feel bad about her past. She'd experienced enough trauma with that to last a lifetime.

After she showered, he helped her place new bandages, and they headed out to the store. She had on a hat and sunglasses, which she said were because of the black eyes and scratches, but he knew she didn't want to be recognized.

They were on the frozen aisle when someone came up behind them. "Hey, I thought it was you. How are you doing?"

Talia froze beside him, but she didn't need to worry. It was one of the SEALs who'd retired recently and they were talking to him.

Zip turned and shook Wolf's hand. Talia still looked wary, so he gently put his arm around her and pulled her closer. "Wolf, this is Talia."

Wolf's eyes narrowed an almost imperceptible amount as he took in Talia's injuries. He recovered fast and shook Talia's hand. "It's nice to meet you. Caroline is coming around the—there she is." He waved his wife over, and she didn't bat an eye as she shook Talia's hand while Wolf introduced her.

"It's nice to meet you. Have you and Zip been together long?"

"Um…"

Talia didn't know how to answer that question, so Zip changed the subject. "Did you two enjoy your trip?"

Wolf and Caroline both nodded. "Very much. Why don't you all come over next weekend?" Caroline asked.

Zip hadn't ever been invited over to Wolf's house. Caroline wasn't just smart, she had emotional intelligence and the desire to care for injured women. He'd heard about how she took different women under her wing and helped them. It would be something special for Talia. Plus, being invited into Wolf's inner sanctum was special.

"Sure. That would be very nice of you," Zip said. He wasn't sure Wolf wanted him over, but he knew the man trusted his wife.

"Thank you. Are you sure?" Talia asked.

Zip knew her hesitation was more about protecting strangers from her past than a lack of desire to go.

"Yes, very sure," Caroline said.

"I'll call you this week with the details," Wolf said.

Zip pulled out his phone. "I don't know that you have my number."

Wolf chuckled. "If I don't have it, I can get it."

Zip didn't doubt for a moment that Wolf could get everything on him in a matter of hours. The man was a legend, and everyone wanted to work with him or be friends. It didn't take a rocket scientist to know it was always best to stay on Wolf's good side.

"Awesome, we'll see you next weekend."

He finished shopping with Talia, and they were in the car on the way home when she spoke up.

"So that guy, Wolf, he said he could get your number. How can he do that?"

"He used to be a SEAL, and he's friends with a lot of people."

"So you don't think he'll try to get a background check on me, right?"

They were almost home, so he waited to answer until they pulled into the driveway and stopped the car. "If Wolf ever found out, I can guarantee he would never hold it against you. He's not that kind of man."

Talia scoffed. "Most guys are that type of man."

"Well, Wolf isn't. He would never hold your past against you even if he couldn't tell you were too young to have consented to that stuff."

She sighed and shook her head. He reached over and turned her head so she was looking at him.

"Trust me."

Her shoulders dropped before she nodded. "Okay. I'll trust you. But it's going to be difficult if any of them say anything."

"I know. And they won't. They'll all behave."

"Thank you."

"For what?"

"Being decent."

A little piece of him died inside. She'd been through so much shit all because of her sister. It was time Talia experienced something good. And he wanted to be the man to deliver it to her.

19

Talia was getting too used to having Zip around in the evenings. She wasn't back at work yet, but she would have to go back soon. Her bills wouldn't pay themselves, and she needed money.

It sucked that she did all that work as a teen and never got paid a dime. Since she was the one who earned the money to buy her sister's bar, she should own part of it, but she feared telling authorities about her past. They didn't like people who did porn, even if it had been forced on them.

Besides, her sister had threatened arrest if the cops ever found out. It seemed silly now, but when she could have sued her sister, she'd been too afraid.

Now, she was sure whatever limitations on time would have passed.

"Hey, Talia, I'm home," Zip called out as he entered the house. She liked that he called out when he came in. It made her feel safe.

She stepped out of the bedroom and froze. He had a bruise on the side of his face. "What happened?"

"Nothing much. We were doing training and I ended up getting hit. I'm okay."

"Hit by what?"

"Just some stuff. Nothing big. It happens."

She moved to him and lifted her hand but didn't touch his face. "It looks bad."

"I know. But it's not awful. I'll be fine."

"You look worse than I did."

He rolled his eyes, then looped his arm around her and pulled her close. "It's not a competition. I'm fine. I'll be fine. Just need to take it easy for a few days."

"Caroline called today."

"Really?"

"Yes. I was surprised she could get my number so easily. She asked if we were free on Saturday. I said yes since I won't be back at work yet."

"Good. I think you'll enjoy getting together with them."

"I'm sure I will. I also made us dinner. Nothing fancy, just some stew."

"Nice. I'll be out in a few. I just want to change."

"Sure. And I think you should take it easy tonight."

"We both can. How about we find a movie and stretch out on the couch?"

"That sounds nice."

"Good. I'll change clothes, and then we can eat and watch a movie."

Talia checked on the stew and decided it was done. She unplugged the slow cooker and grabbed two bowls. She was about to serve dinner when Zip came back into the room. He looked amazing in his blue t-shirt and sweats. She couldn't help but stare. It was difficult being around someone as good looking as Zip and not watch his every move.

She knew whatever they had wouldn't last. He was nice for now, but after a few more run-ins with over-enthusiastic men, he would tire of the hassle. She might as well enjoy being with Zip while she had the chance.

On Saturday, they headed to Wolf and Caroline's place. She was disappointed she and Zip hadn't had sex, but both of them were still banged up. She worried about him and what had happened. One morning, when she'd been heading to the bathroom, she'd glanced into his room and saw his side, which looked fairly heavily bruised. She hoped he was okay. If she knew him better, she would know if it was safe to question him about it. He hadn't divulged anything to her, so she kept the questions to herself.

Caroline had invited a few other people over, and they were outside on their patio. The weather was perfect, and everyone seemed to be in a good mood.

"Talia, this is Remi and Kevlar."

She shook Kevlar's hand first, then Remi's. "Hi, it's nice to meet you."

"And this is Safe and Wren."

She turned to them and smiled, shaking their hands. "It's good to meet you, too."

Neither Remi nor Wren asked about her fading bruises. She was surprised that all the women were so nice and open. She'd never experienced much female bonding, so them talking to her and including her in their conversations seemed like prime bonding to her. They were all talking about a sale on shorts they'd found out about the day before.

"Talia, do you like to shop?" Caroline asked.

She shrugged. "I don't have much time, and I clean offices after hours for a living, so I don't really have time to wear anything cute."

Remi snorted. "When I'm working, I just wear whatever I have on, which is usually a t-shirt and sweats."

Wren chuckled. "If the clothes are priced well, I like them better."

Caroline nodded. "I do love a bargain."

"Oh no, more bargains," Safe said as he pulled Wren up and kissed the side of her cheek. "Tell me where, and I'll go buy it for you."

Talia liked how the guys were teasing and having fun with their women, but the teasing wasn't mean. They got along, which impressed her. She wondered if it would ever be as easy with her and Zip.

Later, after they'd eaten, she stepped out of the bathroom and ran right into Zip. She might have let out a small yelp, but it was overshadowed by Zip's grunt. She narrowed her gaze, taking him in. "You're more injured than you told me." He opened his mouth, but she held up one finger and shook her head. "Do not lie to me."

"I'm fine, or I will be. I'm taking it easy for a few days."

"What happened?"

He shrugged and her frown deepened. He let go a heavy breath and shook his head. "We were doing an exercise and a piece of equipment broke. I fell and hit my side on the building."

"What the hell? Something broke?"

"Yeah. And it wasn't because someone did something wrong. It really was something that broke and no one was prepared for it. I'll be fine."

"Let me see."

He shook his head. "Not right now. When we get home."

She couldn't force him. He was much stronger, and they were at his friend's place. Later, she would make him show her the injury.

After another twenty or thirty minutes, they said goodbye and headed out. She was ready to find out exactly how injured he was.

Once back at his place, she stood in the entryway and put her hands on her hips. "How bad is that injury?"

"Really, it's not that big of a deal."

"Let me look."

He rolled his eyes and then pulled up his shirt, exposing a bruise. She moved to him and put her hand on his side. He winced, and she pulled back.

"That is significant. Why didn't you tell me? You've been doing so much for me, and I could have—"

"I'm fine."

She shook her head. "You should have let me help."

"I didn't want to bother you."

She pursed her lips together. "It wouldn't have been a bother."

He cupped her face. "I'm sorry. I should have said more about it, but I really didn't want you to worry."

"Why not? You're worried about me."

He opened his mouth and then closed it. "I guess no one has ever really been worried about me before. I mean, the guys, sure, but they all know I can handle myself. I was able to catch myself when the equipment failed."

She took him by the hand and led him to the couch. "Tell me about it. I want to know everything."

Zip couldn't believe Talia wanted to hear about

what happened. Before, when he'd been with a woman, they hadn't wanted to hear about his life. With Talia, it was different. She wanted to know about him.

"It was a routine training. Nothing should have gone wrong. I was two stories up on a climb, and the anchor we were using broke. It had been checked over multiple times by different members of the team. All of us were using it, and it was my turn. It broke. I fell about ten feet, caught myself, and then landed hard on my side."

"Shit. You told me you were hit by equipment."

"Really, it's not a big deal."

She held his face so he was looking at her. "It is a big deal. You could have fallen and broken something."

His eyes burned, and he wanted to look away, but the intensity in her gaze drew him in closer. His lips hovered next to hers and she closed the distance. He didn't pull her too close, and she didn't squeeze him.

He thought the kiss would end, and that would be that. Then Talia pulled her shirt off, and he lost his mind at the sight of her breasts barely covered by some thin, lacy material that begged him to touch.

His gaze stayed on her breasts for ten, maybe fifteen seconds, as his cock grew hard. When his gaze lifted to hers, he saw fear. He cupped her cheek, wanting to assure her she wasn't doing anything wrong.

"You're so freaking beautiful."

"I want to see you."

He slowly drew in air through his nose then nodded before he ripped his shirt off. Her fingers were like feathers over his skin. He moaned, and she reached down to the button of his shorts.

"I want you. I don't want to put it off."

He nodded. "I don't want to hurt you."

She shook her head as she ran her fingers over his shoulder. "You won't. We'll be careful."

Her touch sent sparks along his skin. "I want to shower. I don't want to stink."

"You don't stink."

"Still, I want to be clean."

"Let's shower together."

He couldn't believe he was lucky enough to be with this beautiful woman. He let her use the restroom first and get into the shower. She seemed a little shy when he entered the stall, but it didn't take too long for them both to relax.

They weren't getting out of the shower until he

got her warmed up. When he first slid his fingers down her belly to her pussy, she sucked in air. He paused.

"This okay?"

She nodded. "Yes. I just don't want to disappoint you."

He shook his head. "You won't."

She ran her hands down the side of his body and around to his butt. "What do you like?"

"I like sinking my dick into a hot pussy. But first, I want to get you off. I want you to be so ready for me, you're begging."

"Oh."

He laughed, then ran his hands down to her pussy, sliding his fingers over her slit. He liked the way she moaned and how her body jerked against him. Imagining her underneath him was driving him crazy.

Talia couldn't believe how good Zip was. He was touching her exactly how she liked it. His fingers on her clit felt like she was doing it for herself but better. The thought of him being the one touching and driving her closer to orgasm heightened her enjoyment.

"More," Talia cried out when he slid his fingers into her and grazed her clit with his thumb. She threw her head back and gasped as he pushed her over the edge. She came hard against his fingers, clinging to him as she lost herself to him.

When she recovered, she wrapped her fingers around his cock, but he grabbed her wrist and stopped her movement. She glanced up and met his gaze.

"I'm not going to last if you touch me."

"Oh."

"Yeah, I'm on edge and about to fall over. You're so fucking hot, and I want to be inside you."

His words made her shiver. "I want that, too. But we have to use a condom."

He nodded, and she thought about relenting, but she'd never had sex without a condom. She needed at least that one little piece of assurance.

"I have plenty of condoms in the bedroom."

"Good. How about we dry off and get in there?"

He shut off the water and grabbed a towel for her. She couldn't believe how good it felt being with Zip. It was like they were meant to be together.

Sex had never meant so much to her. She'd been used and didn't have great memories of sex. But with Zip, it was different. He made her feel good, like she was special. That was the biggest difference. She felt special with him.

Zip stood above Talia as she spread out on his bed. She'd been sleeping in his guest room on the futon, but this was where he'd wanted her. Her pussy was neatly trimmed and looked so inviting. He lowered, grazing his nose along the inside of her knee.

The way her body shivered made his insides tingle. When his lips pressed against her pussy, she gasped. He licked up her slit, forcing his tongue to press harder on her clit. The way she cried out made him even harder.

She tasted so good. He wanted to spend time driving her crazy as he ate her out, but he was too turned on to do everything he wanted. His cock wasn't going to last, and he hoped he didn't embarrass himself when he slid in.

After a moment, he lifted up and met her gaze. "I hope you know this first time isn't going to be indicative of how the tenth time will go."

Her eyebrows lifted. "The tenth?"

"You're freaking hot. Too hot. You make me so turned on it's hard to breathe around you. Sliding into you will be too much."

"I'm ready for you to slide in."

"Good. Because I need to be inside you."

He grabbed the condom, rolling it on. She adjusted her hips and lifted her legs. He moved on top of her, and she wrapped her legs around him, pulling him closer.

He lined up and was ready to slide in when she met his gaze and held it. As he slid in, it felt like he could see into her soul.

She squeezed him, and he gasped, almost losing it all. He had to slow down, or this would be over within less than forty-five seconds. She had him so twisted up he couldn't think straight.

Her hands were on his back, then his ass. They were going at it too hard, and his side ached, but he didn't want to pull back, but he did slow so he didn't hurt her.

"More," Talia said as she squeezed her pussy.

His eyes rolled up as the sensation shot through him like lightning. "You're driving me too wild. I can't last."

"Come. We can do this again later."

"You should come first."

"No, it's—"

He slid his hand between their bodies and found her clit. She gasped and bucked her hips. He needed more time to explore, but he wasn't going to last. She was too hot, too kind, and he was falling for her. He was totally and completely taken in by her. This was the first time they'd had sex, and already he was head over heels. It should be impossible, but maybe this was exactly how it should work.

He pumped in fast, his hips thrusting deep before he stilled, gasping as his body spiraled out of control. She had taken everything, even his soul.

When he opened his eyes, he couldn't believe that she'd allowed him to be with her. "Thank you. That was an incredible experience. I can't believe you are with me."

"I can't believe you want me."

"Every single day. I want you, Talia. I want all of you."

He pulled out and kissed the side of her head before tossing the condom. This was the kind of relationship he vowed never to have, but he never wanted this to end. Talia was the perfect person for him, and he wanted to make sure she knew how much he cared for her.

20

Being with Zip was nearly magical. He cared deeply for her. It was unlike any relationship she'd ever been in. Of course, her past was littered with toxic people and toxic situations. With Zip, everything was better.

She was back at work, which meant she got home close to midnight, so he was asleep and he left early while she slept. The days she didn't work were best. That's when they made love and she realized she had a great man.

Two weeks after the first time they'd had sex, she was at home alone when her phone rang. It was the police. They wanted her to come to the station. She texted Zip as she was driving over.

He called seconds after she stepped into the

station, and she answered. "I just stepped into the station. I'll call you when I get done."

"Are you okay?"

"Yes. They want to talk about the guy who assaulted me. I'm fine."

"Okay. Call if you need something. And if you can't get hold of me, call Caroline and Wolf."

"Okay. Thank you."

She ended the call and was greeted by someone in uniform. "Can I help you?"

"Yes, I'm here to talk to Detective Huett. They called me."

"Sure. I'll tell Huett you're here."

She only had to wait a few minutes before Huett called her back. A woman joined them in the room. "Hello, I'm Amy. I'm here for you, not the police."

"I'm sorry. I don't understand. Are you a lawyer?"

"No, I'm a psychologist."

Huett cleared his throat. "I asked Amy to join us. I—" Huett coughed and glanced down at the table.

Talia's stomach clenched. He knew. There was no way he didn't. Now, they wouldn't take her seriously.

"I wanted you to have support. You're twenty-eight, right?"

"Yes, sir."

"When were you freed?"

She shook her head. "I don't understand your question."

Amy smiled. "Victims of trafficking have seven years to press charges."

She looked from Amy to Huett. "You're pressing charges against me?"

Huett shook his head. "No. We were talking about charging whoever was responsible for what happened to you."

Tears filled her eyes. Was this for real? Years had been spent fearing the police. Would they really listen to her? "They always said you would arrest me."

"No. I'm sorry you didn't know to come to us. I get it. The police can be scary. If I'd known…I don't know. I hoped if I figured out someone was being abused that way at thirteen years old, I would have done something to fight it. I'm sorry you weren't taken care of properly."

Her throat closed, and her heart squeezed. "No one ever cared."

"I do. And I'm sorry you didn't know that. I

didn't make detective until a few years ago, but I hope that if I found you when I'd been a street cop, I would have tried everything I had to get you justice."

Amy gave her a box of tissues and poured some tea from a container she'd missed earlier. She appreciated what they were doing. It wouldn't take away all the years of pain she'd suffered, but knowing someone cared about her made her feel like maybe she was worth something.

After she recovered a little more, Huett assured her they would make the charges against Dave, her new landlord, stick. They were digging to find more people who would testify against him.

This was better than she ever could have imagined. By the time she left the station, she felt better than she had in years.

She sat in her car and sent a text to Zip, telling him everything was great and they could talk when she got home. Excitement filled her, and she drove home carefully, ready to spend the evening in Zip's arms.

21

Zip was ready to head home when his phone buzzed. All the other guys on his team got the same message. Anger and disappointment twisted together. He wouldn't make it home tonight. They were headed out of the country.

He stepped outside and called Talia. When he heard her voice, he closed his eyes, taking in the joy as she explained how the police were doing everything they could to keep Dave in custody.

"Hey, sweetie, I got called out on a mission."

"Wait, what?"

"I know this timing sucks. Please stay at my house. Caroline and Wolf will step in if you need help. Also Kevlar's team isn't heading out, so Remi and Wren will be around. There's a friend, Thario. He's a good person. We were going to get together with him, but he got a cold. I trust him. I'll make sure you have their numbers."

He heard her take a deep breath and let it go. "I'll be fine. And I'll be waiting here for you to get home."

"It could be a week or two. Or maybe a month. I don't know." She didn't say anything for a short moment, and he wondered if he'd lost her. Finally, she spoke.

"That's okay. I'd rather miss you for a few weeks and have you the rest of the time than never have met you."

He closed his eyes, drinking in the sound of her voice. "I know I'm not there in front of you, but I wanted to tell you this weekend, or maybe next, but Talia, I've fallen in love with you."

She gasped. "Oh, Zip. I'm falling for you, too."

"Good. We'll celebrate together when I get home."

"Yes, we will."

He ended that call, glad that he'd called her. She showed him love and kindness. His SEAL brothers were great, but they didn't match what he felt for Talia. It felt like a huge weight had been lifted off his shoulders. They were on the same page, and he couldn't wait to get back and see her.

22

Talia ended the call, happiness filling her. How had everything gotten so good for her? Luck finally seemed to be on her side. She needed to get rid of her apartment, so while Zip was gone and while Dave was still in jail, she would clean it out.

Being at work when Zip was home had started to wear on her. She needed to find something that would allow her to be gone during the day when he was at work. Coming home to him sleeping and him leaving while she was dead asleep was getting old. She would start looking for a different job today.

There were jobs she wouldn't do. Anything customer facing was risky. She'd thought she'd changed enough she wouldn't be recognized, but there were still people like Dave who must have religiously watched the videos she'd been in. Heck, he could have been one of the guys in the videos because thc men hadn't been forced to show their faces and had worn masks. Nothing quite like being abused by masked men.

She pushed away the depressing thoughts and concentrated on what she needed to do to get out of her apartment and start living a better life with Zip.

The list of jobs online was confusing. She'd thought about going with an agency, but she didn't want part of her paycheck to go to someone else. But there were few options. She had to find something good, and it didn't seem like there was anything out there.

She stayed up late researching options for a job, finally deciding to go with an employment agency. The articles she found about agencies promised they wouldn't take her money, so she thought it was worth a shot. Hopefully they wouldn't know about her past and she would be able to get a good job.

The next day she swung by her apartment and started packing things she wanted to keep. She didn't have much, but they were her things and she didn't want to lose them.

When she was almost done, she realized she would have to take a second trip because not everything would fit in her car. For a moment, she thought about calling Caroline and asking if she could help her, but she didn't want to be a bother. She would come back the next day and get more stuff.

Work was boring and coming home to an empty house was depressing. Also arriving at Zip's dark house at midnight was scary. She didn't like coming home this late with no one waiting. Not that his neighborhood was bad, just dark. The houses were older, and some of the neighbors had trees that ate the light. The deep shadows made her wary.

Before going to bed, she pulled the lever on using an employment agency. Hopefully, there would be a job that would allow her to get off earlier in the day so she had more time with Zip.

The next morning she slept late and didn't have time to head over to the apartment before work. Eventually she would make it there, but today was her first day back driving deliveries, and she needed the extra money. Driving deliveries meant she would be busy all day long, but she'd missed so much work, she felt the need to pick up a few hours.

Midway through the day, she checked her email and saw that she had three interviews at the end of the week. Maybe one of those jobs would pan out, and she could stop getting home at midnight. Being with Zip had given her hope, and that hope had convinced her she would find a better job. Once she wasn't working until midnight, she and Zip could make a better future together. At least she hoped they could.

23

Zip allowed himself to think about Talia on the flight overseas, but once they landed, he switched off that part of his brain. Talia would be home once he returned, but to make sure he returned, he had to turn it all off.

They were getting briefed, then would load into a helicopter and fly out to a carrier where they would load into their rubber raiding rafts and sneak into the country. Their operation was risky, but most SEAL operations were.

After going through the steps one more time on the aircraft carrier, they loaded onto the rafts, thankful they had skilled boat operators who could get them exactly where they needed to go, almost to the inch of where they asked to land.

They were headed inland about ten miles and would make their attack close to morning. They'd contemplated going in on a helicopter, but their target would run if they knew anyone was after them. There wasn't an option to fly in closer. This guy was bad and had to be taken out.

After they'd run almost the entire distance, they paused to rest. Back home, Kevlar's team was watching

Rider came over and sat next to him. "You ready?"

Zip nodded. "Sure am."

"Good. Hop said he's set. You two are going in first."

Zip stood and stretched. He and Hop would set up on a hill and provide sniper fire. A part of him wanted to be in on the action, but not everyone could go in close.

Hop nodded as he approached, and they took off together, going the last half mile quickly. They were set up in less than five minutes, and the rest of the team followed. He watched, ready to take out anyone who put up resistance.

"Looks like you have two tangos coming in fast from the west. Driving a van," Kevlar said over coms.

Zip was glad Kevlar's team was on overwatch. It helped when they had guys they trusted watching their back.

"Got it," Hop said.

Zip kept his eyes on the compound as Hop adjusted and fired one round, stopping the van dead in its tracks. There wasn't time to celebrate because their team was moving in.

Zip saw someone on the north side of the complex moving fast. He took the guy out. Blink was informing their guys moving in that someone was on the east side.

"Got it," Hop said over coms.

They were moving parts of one machine dedicated to the mission. He trusted his crew to get the job done. They were the best of the best, and Bud, Trip, Rider, and Q proved it with how fast they moved in and took care of the target. He and Hop took out enemy combatants as they scurried away. A few of them raced to the area where his team was located, but with Kevlar's team on watch, he and Hop were able to keep everyone safe.

Getting out would be just as difficult as getting there had been, but now the sun would be up. They planned to move unless someone learned of their activities and followed them.

The team was almost back, and Hop put away his sniper equipment first, then Zip took care of his. It would take more time to leave than it had to arrive. It was just how missions like this went. They would have to be careful and not get caught.

He was sure people living in the surrounding area knew something had gone down. Hopefully, none of them were the curious type.

Once he had his equipment put away, they took off with Kevlar's team still watching. They'd gone about a mile when the warning went out. A group of armed men in trucks were headed their way. They would have to find somewhere to hunker down and wait until darkness. Out here in the open, they were sitting ducks. They just had to keep their heads on a swivel and pray nothing went bad.

24

Talia woke up early and headed to her old apartment, ready to finish her move. She hadn't unpacked anything just in case Zip wanted her to actually live somewhere else. She didn't think he wanted that, but they hadn't discussed where she would go once she felt better.

The apartment had been her slice of freedom. Moving here had meant something. Too bad her landlord's son was a prick. There was no way she could stay, not after what he'd done.

After loading her last box, she went upstairs and took one last look around. She had a letter ready to stuff in the drop box at the front door of the restaurant and would shove her keys in there, too. No way would she ever come back here. Dave could just be mad once he learned she had moved out.

She was about to walk out the door when it swung open. Fear shot through her before she turned. Then she spun and saw her sister standing in the doorway. The fear turned to anger.

"What are you doing here?"

Cheryl didn't move, instead she looked her up and down. "I finally figured out how to get rid of you."

"You can't get rid of me."

"Too bad. I've already arranged it. I was just looking for the right time."

Cheryl looked and sounded too confident. Something was going down, and Talia wanted no part of it.

"Just leave. I have friends who will be here soon."

Cheryl threw her head back, laughter spilling out. "No, you don't. You have no friends, and no one is coming to save you."

Cheryl stepped closer, causing Talia's throat to close with fear.

"Walk out and leave me alone. I'm warning you." Though Talia's words were fierce, her voice shook.

Her sister threw back her head and laughed more. "You are too funny."

The door opened behind Cheryl and Talia watched in disbelief as two men stepped in. These guys were much bigger than her and even if she fought hard, she couldn't overpower both of them. No question, her future with Zip was over.

25

Zip stood in the shower, washing the grime from their mission off his body. He couldn't wait to get home to Talia. It would take them a few days to make it home, but at least they were headed that way. He wanted nothing more than to pull her close and hold her. He hoped they returned home on a day she didn't have to work.

"You in here, Zip?" Rider called out.

"Yeah. Just finishing."

He turned off the water and grabbed a towel. "What's up?"

"Nothing much. Just checking on you. We're leaving in about an hour. Got a ride out for us."

"Awesome. I'm ready to get home."

"Oh yeah, Talia. How is that working out?"

"Excellent."

Rider laughed. "That's too funny. You were one of the ones who wasn't going to fall. But I could almost hear the slam of you hitting the ground."

He snapped his towel. Almost hitting Rider, who laughed even more. "Yeah, she's got me. No question, I've fallen for her. I'm happily joining the crowd of happily paired off. What about you?"

Rider shrugged. "I'm fine alone. But if I find someone, that would be great, too."

"Look at you, all in touch with your inner self."

Rider chuckled. "Keep it up, buddy, and I'll make sure Talia knows you're mooning over her."

"Tell her. I'm fine with that."

"Oh, how the mighty fall," Q said as he entered the room.

Zip smiled, happy to take their joking. They were right. He had fallen hard for Talia. "You ready?" he asked as he pulled on his shirt.

"Yeah. We're ready," Q said as he followed Zip out the door.

After a mission, the pressure was off. He liked this feeling. Success was nice. He'd never been on a total failure of a mission. They'd made mistakes before, but nothing had ever been a failure. He wasn't sure how his buddy Sharp had dealt with the mission he'd been on that had failed. That had to have been terrible. Losing friends like he had must have been a real mind fuck. They didn't talk about it, but he knew from the few things Sharp had said it had screwed him up. He wouldn't wish that on anyone.

Going home felt good. Much more special knowing Talia would be there for him. He never wanted to forget this feeling.

* * *

TALIA REACHED FOR HER PHONE, but her sister knocked it from her hand before she could use it. She tried to get the digital assistant to call emergency services, but Cheryl screamed so loud the assistant couldn't hear her.

"Shut up, you bitch! You're never getting free of me."

"Help!" Talia tried to run around Cheryl, but two men were on the stairs. She was trapped. There was no way for her to escape. "Help!" she screamed again, hoping someone heard.

Cheryl's hand landed on her cheek, sending pain straight through her and dropping her to her knees. One of the guys stepped inside and grabbed her by the hair, yanking her backward.

"Stop!" He held her in an awkward position, her back arched, her legs bent awkwardly. She couldn't catch her breath. Tears streamed down her face. "Leave me alone."

Cheryl knelt beside her, disdain clear in her eyes. "No can do. You used to be helpful."

"Just stop," Talia begged.

"No. I don't think so." Cheryl stood and waved for the men to follow with her. "Come now. We have work to do."

The guys grabbed her, and though she tried to fight them, it was no use. They had too good of a hold on her. She wasn't going to get free. She knew what would happen, how it would go from here on out. Her life was over, and there wasn't anything she could do to change that.

Zip stored his equipment and headed to his truck, ready to see Talia. She hadn't texted him and he was a little worried about her lack of communication, but he knew they were solid. She was probably busy or something and hadn't wanted to bother him. He appreciated her thoughtfulness.

He pulled up at his house, a little surprised her car wasn't there. He stepped inside and paused. The place didn't seem like she'd been there in a while. There was coffee left in the pot. He moved to the kitchen and emptied it, thinking it was weird that she had left coffee in there. That wasn't like her. She always cleaned up before she left for work. It was one of those things he told her she didn't have to do, but she couldn't stop herself from doing based on past experiences.

He moved to the bathroom and saw all her stuff still there. She hadn't brought over everything, but her hair and face stuff was still on his bathroom counter.

Zip moved through the house, opening each door. He found boxes in the spare room and opened the top one. It seemed to be filled with her clothes. He froze, thinking what it meant.

She had gone back to her place and moved her things here. Where was she now?

He pulled out his phone and dialed. It rang through to voicemail. Worry hit hard. This wasn't good at all. Deep in his soul, he knew something bad had happened.

He called Thario, hoping his buddy had some scrap of information he could give him. Maybe he was overreacting, but he didn't think so.

"Hey, Zip, what's up?"

"I don't know."

"That doesn't sound good."

"I think something is wrong."

"Tell me."

"Talia isn't here. Something happened."

"She's the one you thought about giving the tracking earring to?"

"Yes. But she didn't like the idea of being watched. I get it. I don't like being tracked either but sometimes it's necessary and I didn't do enough to explain who you were and what you would use tracking for."

"Let me see what I can find. I'll call you when I get some information."

Zip glanced around, worry growing with each minute. "Okay. Mind if I come over?"

"Come on."

"I'll bring a pizza."

"Make it sausage and black olive."

"Got it. I'll be about thirty minutes."

Zip hung up and wrote a note to Talia, asking her to call if she came home. He glanced back at the kitchen, trying to decide if he was overreacting or if his feelings that something was off were real. It felt real. She wouldn't have left the coffee in the pot. Worry filled him as he stepped out. She was in trouble. He placed an order for the pizza before he pulled out of the driveway. Worry hung heavy. He hoped he could find her. He didn't think she'd left on her own. Her hair stuff was there, along with her face cream. She loved that face cream. Said it was the one luxury she never would give up. Something had gone wrong.

He picked up the pizza, resisting the urge to call Thario. He was busy working, and he didn't need Zip interrupting him. It took all his restraint to keep from calling and asking if Thario had found something.

When he knocked at Thario's door, Frog gave a small bark that sounded almost muted. The door opened, and Frog was there wagging his tail alongside Thario.

"That smells great. I've got some information. Not sure you're going to like it."

"Tell me as I get us some pizza. How many slices do you want?"

"Two to start."

Thario moved to his desk and sat, groaning. Zip worried about his buddy. It had to be hard navigating everything. Thario had been a ladies' man before the bomb that had blown his legs off. Now, women didn't want anything to do with him. Zip wasn't sure how to help, or if there even was a way to help Thario. He should come around more just to hang out.

Zip turned to face him. "The jerk who beat her up, her new landlord, he's still in jail. It wasn't him.

Her sister is living her life like everything is normal. There's nothing new going on with her, so I don't think she took Talia. I have no leads, and I don't like that. I can't pin anything down."

"Fuck. I don't know what to do. I don't know where she is."

"I'll keep looking. Don't give up."

He took a bite of the pizza, thinking it wasn't as good as he thought it should be. If Talia was here, he knew it would taste great. Everything was better with her around.

After he swallowed his next bite, he spoke up. "I'm going to head to her old apartment and see if I can figure out anything."

"I'd go with you, but my legs are about to give out for the day."

"No worries. You need to take care of yourself. You're too important of a friend."

"Thanks. And I want to meet her when she comes home. I know last time I got sick, and you two couldn't come over."

"How do you feel now?"

"My lungs are better. I'm just tired. My legs hurt today. I might have overdone it."

"Take care of yourself. You're a friend, not just someone who helps. I would hate to lose you."

Thario's eyes darted away for just a second, then swung back to Zip. "Thank you. You guys keep me sane."

Zip squeezed his shoulder, then patted Frog on his head. "Thank you. I'll text you about what I find."

"Be safe. You don't have backup."

Zip shut the door behind him, wondering if he should call backup. Everyone was tired after their mission. He was exhausted but had to look for Talia. She wouldn't have just wandered off. Or would she? He didn't really know her. Maybe she was fine and had just taken off with some guy for a long weekend. But that didn't seem like her.

He was mixing himself up. There had to be more to her not being around. She wouldn't have run off without him. That wasn't her. He owed it to her to find out what had gone down. She deserved at least that much.

27

Zip glanced down, seeing that his tank was almost empty. He had to waste time and stop for gas. He hated that he hadn't filled up before the mission. He should have known he would need to fill up at the worst time imaginable.

He pulled into a gas station, cursing himself all the while. He hated that he was wasting time. Maybe he could have made it to Talia's place, but he wasn't sure. And if he had to go somewhere after, there's no way he could drive anywhere else.

As he was scanning his credit card, a car pulled up next to him. He didn't pay the person any mind and was surprised when they stepped to his side of the pump.

"Zip, I'm surprised to see you out. Didn't you just get home from a mission?"

"Hey, Kevlar. Yeah, we just got home."

"Aren't you tired? What are you doing out? Should you be sleeping?"

Zip shook his head, wondering if he should get into it. "I don't know. I can't find my girl, and I'm worried."

Kevlar sobered. "Wait, she's missing? How long?"

"It's going to sound stupid, but I came home, and she wasn't there. All her stuff was there, but she left coffee in the pot."

Kevlar narrowed his eyes, and his lips thinned. "Could she just have forgotten it?"

Zip shook his head. "I know it sounds stupid. The cops would laugh me out of the place if I went to them. That's why I'm heading over to her old apartment to see if she's there."

"I'll go with you. Let me fill up, and I'll pull out right behind you."

"You don't have—"

"Nonsense. If your woman is missing, I'm not abandoning you. I'll text Remi and tell her I'm helping you."

"As long as it's not a bother."

"Buddy, even if it was a bother, I'd help you."

"Thanks, man."

He was thankful he'd run into Kevlar. They might not find anything, but at least he had backup now.

28

Talia squeezed her knees closer, wishing she'd waited to clean out her apartment. Her sister had her locked in a room with no windows. She wasn't sure exactly where she was, but because of the loud music, she had a suspicion that it was the bar. It could be anywhere, but the bar fit. The loud music was either cover to keep her screams from being heard, or it was just the bar.

She wouldn't survive this again. She knew what was coming. No question, her life was over. Her sister wouldn't let her escape this time. She would be used up until the last drop of her soul was gone.

After an hour or maybe minutes later, the door opened. Cheryl stepped in, followed by one of the men who'd held her in the back of the car when she'd been taken.

Hate filled her. She wanted to get up and beat the shit out of her sister. She knew she wouldn't make it to Cheryl without the asshole behind her attacking and taking her down.

"I'm going to make sure you are taken care of. You'll never darken our door again. You've been a blight on this family from the day you were born."

"Why do you hate me so much you have to destroy me?"

"Because you ruined everything. You ruined every day of my life after you came home from the hospital with my mother. You took her, and you made me the bitch I am today. This is your fault."

Talia had never understood why her sister hated her so. She'd just been a kid and nothing more, then her sister's twisted imagination had ruined their relationship. Jealousy. That was the only explanation for Cheryl's behavior. She'd wanted to be the queen of the family but had been upstaged by a baby girl.

They could have been friends, or at least had a halfway decent relationship, but Cheryl had ruined it. Now, they were enemies, and that would never change.

"What are you going to do?"

"I'm looking into options. You'll probably end up shipped overseas. I think that will get me the most money. I have to get rid of you. That's the only option. You can't live around here any longer."

Talia shook her head. "You're pathetic."

Cheryl stalked over and backhanded her, sending pain through her face and down her neck. She jerked up, but the guy was on her, punching her in the face and knocking her on her ass.

The punches hurt but the worst part of this was that she'd never get the chance to say goodbye to Zip. He would think she'd just wandered off and left him. He wouldn't know she'd been taken against her will. She wanted a life with Zip. She wanted to be his. It made her so sad that their relationship would only exist in her mind, nothing else.

Zip pulled up outside the restaurant where Talia's apartment was located and spied her car. His heart picked up speed, and he waved Kevlar over. "That's her car."

"She lives upstairs?"

"Yes."

"Let's go. Maybe she's just up there asleep."

He hoped she was up there going through her stuff or taking a nap but knew she wasn't here. She would have called or texted. There wasn't any way she would have stayed here, not after what had happened with her new landlord.

When he got to the top of the stairs, he tried the door and found it open. "That's concerning."

Kevlar nodded. "Let me guess, there's no way she would have left it unlocked."

"No way."

They stepped in and paused. Kevlar pointed to the phone on the floor. "Is that hers?"

"Fuck."

"Don't touch anything. We should call the cops."

Zip pulled out his phone and checked for a message from Talia, but he didn't find one. Kevlar was right. They had to call the police. She was missing.

Before the police arrived, he and Kevlar had time to look for anything that would tell them what had happened. It looked like Talia had boxed up the rest of her stuff. She'd probably been here to clean out her place and move the rest of the boxes to his house.

"Is she moving?" Kevlar asked.

"Moving in with me."

"You two haven't known each other long."

"No, and she'd been sleeping in my guest room on the futon, but we were getting closer, and I told her I was in love with her before I left on the mission. She said it back to me. Everything was going great."

Kevlar nodded. "I don't like this. Who would want to hurt her?"

Zip blew out a breath. "Her sister."

Right then, the cops showed up. They made a note about the phone on the floor and the boxes. One of the officers raised his eyebrows and shook his head.

"Where were you this last week?"

"On a mission." Zip couldn't believe this was happening.

"Where exactly?" the officer asked.

Zip shrugged. "Sorry, it's classified."

The officer raised his eyebrows and was about to say something when Kevlar spoke up. "He was out of the country. We should probably call one of the Jags."

"Oh," the officer said. "She wasn't military, was she?"

Zip sighed and shook his head slowly. "No, sir. But her sister is awful."

The officer looked up from his notepad and narrowed his gaze. "What do you mean awful?"

"This is a long story. She was talking to a detective." He squeezed the bridge of his nose with his thumb and forefinger. "The detective's name is Hyatt."

"You mean Huett?"

He nodded. "Yes. Huett. That's who she was talking to. He knows some of the stuff going on."

"Let me call him."

The officer stepped away, and Kevlar came closer. "You okay?"

"Not really. Listen, there's something bad." He put his hands on his hips and blew out a breath. "She had some really bad things that happened in her past. Her family pushed her into it. Some shit is going to come out."

"How bad?"

"People are going to talk and say shit about her."

"I'll shut that shit down fast. She's family."

Relief slid through Zip. His friends really were great. "Thanks, man."

The officer came over as he shoved his phone into his pocket. "Huett is coming by. He is having Dave's visitation and call log checked. Said to canvas and ask neighbors, but this isn't a huge residential area. There are only about eight apartments occupied in this area. We'll figure this out."

"Thank you."

"We'll find her."

Zip didn't want to tell this officer that he knew

the statistics, knew just how many people were found. He sent a text to Thario, telling him what they knew, which wasn't much.

Kevlar squeezed his shoulder. "You need to tell your team and CO. They need to know."

"Thank you, man, for being here. You can go. There's not much more I can do."

"I'm not leaving yet. I'll wait until the detective gets here and they have some idea what their next moves are. Also, if she's still missing, I think we should get a group together this weekend and see what we can find."

"Thank you. You're a good friend."

Kevlar squeezed his shoulder. "We have to be. That's what makes teams strong."

Zip knew what happened with Kevlar and Howler. The betrayal had been a punch to the gut. It had caused some SEALs to leave and others to grow closer. He was lucky his team took it as a sign to be even closer to each other. They would support him through this. He just had to ask for their help.

Talia needed to escape. Her sister was crazy and wouldn't let her go. If she ever wanted to be free, she would have to make it happen.

The door opened, and Cheryl stepped in. Talia was too tired to be angry yet again. She stared up at her sister, wondering what kind of shit she was going to spew today.

"I found you a home. You won't like it, but whatever. You're headed to Asia."

She needed a way to get free. There was no way her sister would allow her out again. Any escape would be over her own making. She would have to outwit her sister and find a way to get free.

"When?"

Cheryl knelt next to her. "In a few days. We're going to move you tonight after the bar closes. You need to be on your best behavior. I'll have four guards with me, so don't even think about escaping. You're worth too much money for me to lose you."

She would have to get free then. Her life would be pain if her sister's plans succeeded.

Cheryl stood and left the room, locking the door. Talia closed her eyes, ready to give up. But she couldn't, not yet. She had to get back to Zip. He was the best thing she'd ever found, and she wanted that again.

Talia circled the room, looking for even the smallest scrap that would help her get free. Cheryl had cleaned the space out. She wondered where the stuff that normally sat in here was. How long had her sister been planning this? Months or years? The plans had to have been in the works for a long time.

She slid down the wall, pulling her legs in close. She was so screwed. She just hoped Zip knew she loved him and would get back to him if she could.

ZIP HAD no clue how to find Talia. The police were planning on questioning her sister, but they needed more than just a hunch that Cheryl had Talia held captive somewhere. Calling the cops had been the right thing to do, but they moved at a snail's pace.

He was going to Thario's place this evening. Thario had been in contact with Tex. Together, they were narrowing down the possible places Talia could be. He knew her sister was involved but confronting her would only make things worse. They had to figure out Talia's location before they went in hard against her sister.

Zip drove to Thario's and saw three cars parked out front. The guys had been taking shifts working with Thario to locate Talia. He appreciated every-thing they were doing, but it seemed like nothing was really happening.

He stepped inside and saw Hop, Kevlar, and Smiley sitting at computers, going through informa-tion. Thario was on the phone, nodding. Frog glanced at him but didn't get up from his place beside Thario.

Zip's throat closed a little as emotions rose. He knew Hop would be there, but he really appreciated the time Kevlar and Smiley were giving to the search. These guys were the best.

Thario ended his call and met Zip's gaze. "I think I have a lead."

His muscles tightened as his head began to buzz. "Really?"

Thario nodded and turned to his computer. He pulled up a secure browser and typed in some information. A map came up, and he leaned in, looking over Thario's shoulder.

"What are we looking at?" Hop asked.

"There is a boat leaving from this location at around midnight. It's about an hour away from us, maybe less, depending on traffic."

"Let's go!" Excitement ripped through Zip.

"Hold up. The informant isn't someone I know. He's into doing some illegal shit and isn't one hundred percent trustworthy."

Zip squeezed his hands into fists. "What percent do you give this information being truthful?"

Thario shrugged. "I'd say sixty. The guy is mad at Cheryl. That means it could be closer to eighty percent correct."

Kevlar pulled out his phone. "How about I call a few guys to go with you? I'm making progress here on the computer."

"I'll go," Smiley said.

Zip nodded. "Let me call Trip and Bud.

Hop stood. "There is no way I'm sitting this out."

"I'll shoot you the address. You'll need to go in ready for anything."

"Got it," Zip said. He would do whatever he had to do to rescue Talia. She was the most important person in his life, and he wouldn't let her slip away.

Talia was tired, but she wouldn't stop resisting Cheryl and the assholes helping her sister until she was dead. Days had passed, and they hadn't allowed her any food, only water. Her stomach had cramped so much she wasn't sure if she could stand up straight.

She missed Zip. Maybe she was building him up in her mind, but she didn't think her memories were that far off. She hadn't hallucinated yet but figured that would come soon enough. If only she could escape into dreams, but the pain in her belly kept waking her every few hours.

A key sounded in the lock, and she backed up, giving herself space to see what was coming at her.

Maybe they were bringing food. Just the thought of food made her stomach rumble. She crossed her arms over her chest and pulled her legs up, trying to make herself as small as possible. It was no use because there was nowhere to hide in the empty room.

The overhead light flipped on, burning her eyes. She blinked a few times before she could make out her sister, followed by two men. She couldn't tell if they were the same two men as earlier since they had on hoodies. But did it matter? None of them would help her.

"Time's up," Cheryl said.

She shook her head. "What do you mean?"

One of the guys came at her, and out of some self-preservation instinct, or maybe it was just hunger, she opened her mouth and clamped down on his arm as he reached for her. Her jaws tight-ened around his flesh, sinking in, drawing blood.

The man screamed, but she didn't let up. It took him four, maybe five seconds to get in a good enough punch to knock her loose. When she let go, he hit her again, knocking her to the floor.

"You fucking bitch!" he roared as he swung his leg back to kick her in the head.

By some miracle, Cheryl stopped him. Maybe her sister felt something, or maybe it was the money she would get by selling her. Cheryl didn't explain. Instead, she directed the men to carry her outside.

Before they got her in the trunk, Talia clipped one of them in the nose with her foot. She'd drawn blood twice. If her body was found, and some police department decided to do some sort of DNA testing, they would find something. She didn't have a chance to get blood from her sister, but maybe one of these two would turn on her and tell the cops about how awful Cheryl really was.

Talia pushed away the fantasy as the car engine rumbled to life. Riding in the trunk wasn't comfortable. Every bump of the road jostled her. She couldn't get a good hold to brace herself and there were things rolling around hitting her.

No question, she was heading to her death. Whatever awaited her wouldn't be fun. She needed to escape, but how? Cheryl had the upper hand, and Talia saw no way to regain it.

How could her sister sell her? It was like they weren't even made from the same people. Her siblings were terrible. Though her brother wasn't involved in this escapade, he'd known their sister had forced her into doing porn when she was a teenager and had done nothing about it.

This felt similar. No one could help her, and they never could when she went up against her sister. They could have been friends, maybe not good friends, but they could have gotten along. But no, her sister had to make everything a competition and force the win. If only she'd learned to fight dirty before her sister had started taking advantage of her. Now she was in this situation, and there wasn't anyone who could rescue her.

No way would Zip know where she was. He wouldn't be able to track her down, even if he wanted to. She should have taken him up on the tracking earrings. She wouldn't be in this situation if she had. He could have already found her by now, and she would be at home in his bed.

What if he didn't care that she wasn't around? He would be better off without her. Everyone would be better off. If she was gone, there would be no explaining that she'd been forced to do porn. There'd be no whispers behind her back, or guys coming at her, thinking they could get in a quick one with her because she was a porn star who did it once with twelve guys. They wouldn't even think it was abuse because she'd done it on the screen so many times in their jerk-off sessions.

Tears ran down her cheeks. She hadn't even known she'd been crying. She hated crying about this. All the tears in the world wouldn't save her. Nothing would.

Zip wanted to tell Hop to drive faster, but they were going a little above the speed limit, and the last thing they wanted was to be stopped by the police. Before leaving, they'd made sure their weapons were loaded and had plenty of firepower to take down multiple people.

They didn't want to hurt Talia, so they were planning to go in quiet, and overpower them in stealth. But if things went sideways, they had the ability to drop them where they stood.

"How much farther?" Hop asked.

"Five minutes," Smiley said.

Trip and Bud were in the car behind them. They planned on driving past the entrance and coming to the marina from the west. He was going to hang back until they located Talia. His emotions were high, and the last thing he wanted was to make a critical error.

"We're approaching now," Hop said.

Zip must have been deep in his musings to not notice the last bit of distance they'd traveled. He checked his watch, seeing they had about twenty minutes before Talia was set to arrive. He was ready, or he thought he was. If they hurt her, he would make sure they paid.

The lot seemed deserted as they pulled in, but then another car pulled in right after Hop killed the lights and engine. They'd taken care of the dome light before leaving Thario's place so they wouldn't draw attention.

"They're going for the trunk," Hop said.

"That has to be her," Smiley said. "I'm texting the rest of the guys and letting them know she's here."

"You ready?" Hop asked.

"Yes." Zip was glad the guys were ready to move. They didn't wait until they had confirmation that Talia was in the trunk. Waiting would put them at too big a deficit.

He slowly inched out of the car, not even trying

to close the door. It would make too much noise and alert Talia's captors that he was there.

Hop and Smiley were already out of the car and approaching the group of four. Two men were dragging, half-carrying Talia. Anger rose as he watched her struggle to walk. What had they done to her?

Someone stepped off one of the boats and onto the ramp leading from land out to the boats farther out. The guy was big, and from the glimpse Zip got, it looked like he was going to be a problem.

"We ain't taking damaged goods."

"She'll survive," the woman said.

That had to be Talia's sister. He wanted to hurt the woman and make her pay for being such a freaking jerk to Talia.

"Can she walk? We aren't taking her on this boat if she can't stand on her own."

Zip inched closer. He was about five feet behind Hop but could hear the conversation going on between the trafficker and Talia's sister.

"She can stand. Stand on your own, Talia."

The two guys tried to let go of Talia, but she dipped to her knees. Zip wanted to cheer her on, but he stayed silent as they moved closer. The idiots weren't paying attention because they had five men surrounding them, and not one of them had real-ized it yet.

"We made a deal. She's fine, just a bitch."

The guy shook his head and turned, waving his hand like he wanted nothing to do with them. Zip had no jurisdiction, but the asshole was a trafficker and needed to go down. Of course, the man was a small node in a huge machine. There was no way the boss was picking up women from a marina. Taking him down wouldn't kill the beast, but he wanted to stall them.

"Listen, lady, she isn't standing on her own. She'll die on the way over. We need healthy women, not used-up bitches. Toss her in the ocean. I'm out of here."

"No!"

The shriek was loud and echoed around them. Zip needed to be closer to Talia to get her free. They had moved as close as they could without exposing themselves. It was time to act and get Talia free from her sister.

Zip was about to move when the guy from the boat spun and punched Talia's sister in the face, dropping her to her knees. The move shocked him, but he couldn't stand idle. He had to save Talia.

33

Talia wasn't going to cooperate. If Cheryl wanted her to stand, she sure as heck wasn't going to. The two men beside her gripped her arms tighter, yanking her up, then released her, trying to force her to stand. She wouldn't.

The person they were selling her to didn't want an injured woman. She would play the injured woman part up, making it seem like she wouldn't survive for long.

Cheryl turned to her and growled. The man was arguing with her, telling her sister to leave. When the guy suggested Cheryl toss her into the ocean, Talia's knees went weaker.

When Cheryl screamed, Talia flinched. She couldn't believe Cheryl was acting like such a fool. Then the man spun around and punched Cheryl.

The two men standing beside her jumped back. She half-expected the men to rush toward Cheryl, or maybe attack the guy, but they were moving away, and fast.

Two other men were there and punched the guys who'd stuffed her into the trunk of the car. What was going on?

Riding in the trunk of the car had disoriented her, but everything seemed very odd. So very odd. Why were two men attacking those guys? Was she about to be attacked by these people?

"Talia!"

The voice sounded familiar. Tears filled her eyes as she watched the man from the boat pick up her sister and drag her toward the boat. But she wasn't crying for her sister. The sound of Zip's voice had made emotions rise. Was this for real? Was she really hearing Zip?

She spun, looking for her man, and there he was. Zip knelt beside her. His hands were on her shoulders, pulling her closer.

"Are you okay?"

She nodded. "Zip?"

"I'm here, babe. I've got you. I'm going to carry you. We need to get you out of here."

"My sister."

Zip paused, and she looked over, seeing the boat heading out of the marina. Zip said nothing as he picked her up and carried her away from the boats and into the parking lot.

"What is going on?" she asked.

"We found you. I can't believe we found you."

"Zip. You were looking for me?"

"Of course."

Another guy came over to the car where Zip had stopped. "I'm on the line with the police to report that woman being taken. What is her name?"

Talia turned to look at the guy. She kind of recognized him but wasn't sure. He was one of Zip's friends. Though she knew her sister would never help her, she couldn't be the same kind of asshole as her sister was.

"Her name is Cheryl Mast. She was going to sell me to him."

The other man relayed the information as she hugged Zip tighter. She relaxed against Zip, finally allowing herself to believe the impossible. She'd been found. She'd been saved.

"You came looking for me."

"I found you." Zip kissed her forehead and then the side of her head.

She couldn't hold back the rush of tears. He'd wanted her enough to look for her. If no one else had been there, she might have been taken with her sister. She couldn't form words, but Zip didn't seem to need anything from her. She was here, in his arms, and her sister wasn't going to get her again.

She heard sirens, and the old worry that she would be in trouble hit. But Zip assured her they were coming to help rescue Cheryl and get a statement from her, not arrest her.

Zip had been correct. She was free to leave about an hour later after the woman on the ambulance had checked her out, saying that she wasn't suffering from anything other than just lack of food and exhaustion. She promised the woman she would go to the ER if she got to feeling bad.

The drive to Zip's place would take almost an hour, so they stopped by a drive-through and bought her a burger and fries. She couldn't eat most of it, but she held onto the bag of food as they drove, glad she could nibble as they went.

Once home at Zip's house, she fell into his arms and cried again. He got her into the shower, and she was grateful for the chance to get clean. He held her as she drifted off, keeping her safe.

When she woke the next morning, he wasn't in bed with her. For a second, she feared being rescued had been a dream. But this was his room, and she wasn't being held any longer.

She stepped out of the bedroom, glad to see him at the stove cooking something.

"Hey, you're up. I made pancakes."

She moved to him, hugging his side. "Thank you. Not just for the pancakes, but for everything."

"You're welcome. We need to head over to Thario's and thank him. Also, you need to meet him. He did so much to find you."

Emotions rose. "I'm so thankful for everyone." She picked up a pancake and shoved a bite into her mouth. She moaned as the flavor spread over her tongue. "So good." Zip put three more on her plate and set it on the table. "So I was out of it last night. Who else was there?"

"Trip and Bud, and then Smiley and Hop were in the car with us."

"I need to thank them."

"Everyone on my team spent time looking for

you, along with the guys on Kevlar's team. They put in the hours and found you."

"I want to do something for them and tell them thank you."

"We were thinking about getting together next Saturday for a picnic. We could bring cookies. I'm sure they would be happy to see you."

"Yes. I want to see them, and I want to bring them cookies I buy from a nice bakery. I really appreciate being found. I would be dead if you hadn't been there. I think that guy would have taken both me and my sister." She took a bite of pancake and chewed, shaking her head.

"Something wrong?"

"No. Just wondering what will happen to my sister."

He shrugged. "I don't know. We did all we could. If they find her, they find her. If not, she's lost to whatever hell she planned on sending you to." Zip came over and sat next to her. "I know she's your sister, but I have no compassion for her. She was going to send you to a fate worse than death."

She nodded. "I know. Still, I don't want that for her, but I don't have the energy to do more than what we have. I won't go looking for her. If she's found, good for her. If not, she did this to herself."

He leaned in and kissed her forehead. "You're living here with me, right?"

Laughter bubbled up. "Of course. I want to spend my life with you."

"Good. I don't want to ever lose you."

"I don't intend on getting lost again." She took another bite and then held up her hand. Zip raised his eyebrows as he chewed. "That tracking thing. I need something. Earrings, a watch, maybe something else. I never want anything like that to happen again."

"Sure, babe. I'll make sure I know where you are all the time."

They chatted about plans and getting the rest of her things as she munched on pancakes. After she was full, they headed to Thario's place. She really liked him, and liked his dog, Frog. Thario seemed like a really great guy, and she liked him even more after he explained how he tracked other women and what he would and wouldn't do. He told her he never violated their privacy, but if there was ever a question about their locations, he checked. He also explained that he had a policy about never divulging to anyone else where the women were unless there was an issue with their safety. That his tracking devices were never to be used to spy on people.

She left Thario's place, satisfied with the tracking device he put in her shoes and the earrings she now wore.

Once back at Zip's place, she headed to the bedroom to nap. When she woke, she felt refreshed. After washing her face, she sought out Zip, wanting more than just a few sweet kisses.

When she found him in the den, he glanced up as she pulled off her shirt and pushed her shorts and underwear low. He swallowed and then stood, saying nothing as he moved to her. He picked her up, and they were in the bedroom in seconds.

His lips were on her, teasing her nipples as he found her clit with his thumb. He knew exactly how to touch her to send her to heaven. She arched up, needing more as he kissed his way down her body. Then his tongue stroked over her clit. She cried out with pleasure as he took her to heaven.

He knew exactly how to lick and suck her to get her off, and it only took a few minutes for her to be coming around his fingers. He grabbed a condom and slid in quickly, filling her all the way.

"Talia, I've fallen so in love with you. I want you forever."

"Yes. I love you, Zip. Forever."

They came together hot and fast, neither of them holding back. They would have time together, enough to spend lazy Sunday afternoons exploring each other. She never wanted anything more. Being with Zip was happiness. Together, they would make a great life.

34

Rider knew he'd failed his sister. He'd been young when their mother died and not that much older when their father passed away. He was her only family, and instead of trying to stick around, he'd gone off and joined the Navy.

Sure, he'd sent her money, paid for her degree, and made sure she had food and a place to live for all those years until she could take care of herself, but he'd left. Now, he was about to see her for the first time in about six years, and his stomach felt tighter than it did before a dangerous mission.

The wedding wasn't until Friday, so that gave him three days to hang out and get to know her again, but he wasn't really looking forward to explaining why he'd abandoned her.

He stepped from the rental and grabbed his bag from the trunk, noticing he was the only one entering the hotel with a military bag instead of a traditional suitcase. None of these people were military. None of them would understand him. The next four days would be interesting.

It had been years since he'd spent any considerable time with civilians. Sure, the women he hooked up with weren't military, but they didn't talk much because that's not why he got together with them. With this crowd, there wouldn't be any hooking up. His sister wouldn't be pleased if he fucked one of her friends, then walked away. He would be on better than his best behavior.

"Excuse me," a soft voice said behind him.

He paused and glanced over his shoulder before turning to face the woman. She was short, plump, with green eyes, and brown hair. She was mostly plain looking, but then her lips spread into a wide smile and his heart hammered so hard he wondered if she could hear it.

"Yes?" he asked, trying to keep his voice even.

"You're Emily's sister." Her hands flew to her

face, which was turning redder by the second. "I meant brother. I didn't mean to imply you looked like a woman. You don't. You definitely look like a man. All man." Her eyes went wide, and her mouth fell open. "Oh God, I'm so sorry. I'm fucking this up more. I need to go crawl under a rock."

She was cute, maybe even cuter the more flustered she got. He tried not to laugh, but he knew a chuckle escaped his lips before he replied.

"Yes, I'm Michael, Emily's sister."

"I need you in my room."

He cocked his head to the side, wondering what she meant when she said she needed him.

Her eyes went even wider as her face turned white. "Oh shit. Emily is going to kill me. You probably think I was propositioning you. I'm not. I just have the tuxedo your sister picked up for you. It's in my room, and she wants to make sure it really fits. She took them the measurements you sent, but the guy said there's no way your body is—" Her gaze dipped to his thighs, and he saw her take in a little gasp. "He said your thighs were too big and your waist too small." She waved her hand at him and shook her head. "I mean, you are proportioned very well. Shit, that came out wrong, didn't it?"

"What's your name?"

"My name?"

"Yes. What's your name?"

"Andie, but not with a y."

"Okay, Andie, not with a y. Let me check-in, and I'll—"

"Oh, you're already checked in. Here's your key. The room has been paid for, and I made sure you had some snacks and drinks in the room."

He wasn't sure exactly who had paid for his room, but he hoped it wasn't his sister. She had too much going on to pay for his stuff. He lived lean, very lean when Emily had been in college. That wasn't an issue now.

"Okay. Take me to my room and let me put my bag down, then I can meet you in your room."

"Thank you. And Michael, it's nice to meet you."

He nodded. "My friends call me Rider, not Michael. So maybe call me that because my real name doesn't feel like me."

"Sure, Rider. Let me write that down. My friends just call me Andie. When I say that out loud, I feel stupid. So never mind and just follow me."

He couldn't help but notice Annie's butt as she scurried in front of him. For her short legs, she moved very fast. It was almost like she was jogging.

She showed him to his room, and he realized her room was just down the hall from his. He would be seeing more of her, which would be nice. Not that he would hit on her, but it would be nice to have her around since she was easy on the eyes and made him wonder if settling down could be a good thing.

He finished in his room quickly and headed out to check on his tux. Maybe he should have had Andie bring it down to his room, but he wanted to get an idea of what kind of person she was, and hotel rooms showed a lot about a person.

The door to her room ended up being around the corner. As he approached the corner, he heard something bang against the wall, and then there were words, but they were low and menacing.

He covered the distance in two long steps and was shocked to see some guy with one hand on Andie's throat, the other tangled in her hair.

"Don't forget it," the jerk growled before he moved to shove her head into the wall.

Rider moved fast and had his hand on the jerk's arm, preventing him from moving. The man gasped and loosened his hold on Andie, which Rider took advantage of and made him drop his hold on the woman. Rider moved to stand between them and pushed the jerk away.

"You dumb fuck. She's trash, not even worth sticking your dick into."

Rider wanted to let this guy have it, but he didn't want to end up in jail for assault. If the guy threw a punch, Rider would return in kind and then some, but until then, he would behave.

"Leave." Rider's one word didn't leave anything up for argument, and he noticed the man stepping back.

Andie moved behind Rider, and the guy yelled out, "Good luck with her. She's a cheating whore."

Rider didn't move, didn't say anything. He just stared the man down until he turned away and stalked down the hall to the elevator. Rider flexed his fists, but when Andie's fingers slid over his arm, he released his fists and turned to face her.

He didn't like the red lump developing on the side of her face, nor did he like the red marks on her neck. He wasn't happy about any of it.

"Let's get you into your room and get ice on this. You need a wet washcloth on your neck."

She shook her head. "No, I'm fine. Don't worry about that. I'm okay."

He stopped her from opening the door and held her gaze. "No, you are not okay. That man assaulted you. Do you want to press charges?"

Andie shook her head. "No. It won't do any good."

"Hey, no one should ever treat you that way."

Her gaze fell and not like when she'd been checking him out. She wanted to hide from him. He'd seen some crazy shit, but witnessing American men abuse their girlfriends or even friends was highly disturbing.

Her shoulders straightened, and she flashed him a smile. "Your tuxedo is right in here. Just need to try it on. If you need adjustments, we can have someone come by."

He wanted to tell her to wait, to get more information, maybe go to the cops, but there was something about the look in her eyes that made him stop. She was on the edge, and he didn't want her to fall. Later, he would figure out who the bastard was. No way would he let the guy get away with what he'd done without some repercussions.

**

Get the next book in the series, *Protecting Andie*, *NOW*

.   .   .

IF YOU ARE interested in Thario and Frog, there is more to his story in the Safeguarded by the SEAL series by Julia Bright. If you are interested in Whisper, his story can be found in *Saving Lorelei* by Julia Bright.

Loved by the SEAL

Protecting Ellis

Protecting Vera

Protecting Talia

Protecting Andie (July 2025)

Protecting Clove (Sept 2025)

Protecting Flora (Nov 11, 2025)

Fighting for Home

A SEAL for Candace

A SEAL for Deb

A SEAL for Elise

A SEAL for Trixie

A SEAL for Raven

A SEAL for Liz

Finding Home

Jenna's SEAL

Ashley's SEAL

Becky's SEAL

Sunshine's SEAL

Audrey's SEAL

Carbon's SEAL

Rosalind's SEAL

Special Forces: Operation Alpha

Saving Lorelei

Rescuing Amy

Saving Sloan

Seeking Justice

Justice for Amber

Searching for Keeley

Justice for Oswin

Safety for Eve

SEAL Target

Wild: A Navy SEAL Romance

Jax: A Navy SEAL Romance

Bear: A Navy SEAL Romance

Harry: A Navy SEAL Romance

Andy: A Navy SEAL Romance

Peach: A Navy SEAL Romance

Safeguarded by the SEAL

Protection for Danika

Protection for Nichole

Protection for Rowan

Protection for Asher

Protection for Amelia

Protection for Elowen

<u>Dark Eagle Series</u>

Survive The Fall

Live Past The Edge

Hold on Through the Pain

Endure the Darkness

<u>Storm Corp Series</u>

Determined

Mountain Rescue

Searching For Sophia

Searching for April

Searching for Claire

Searching for Micki

Searching for Chastity

Triple Threat

Vow to Protect

Pledge to Protect

Promise to Protect

<u>Standalone Romance</u>

Acting The Part

All Business

Just One Taste

Unseen Cruelty

ABOUT THE AUTHOR

Julia Bright is the USA Today Bestselling author of the contemporary military romance Dark Eagle series and is an Operation Alpha Author. Julia lives in the south where "bless your heart" is an insult and "shut up" shows love. Julia has been reading since they could open a book and has taken the passion for words and combined it with the love of travel to create stories full of passion and excitement. If you love a good book with a fantastic happily ever after, you'll enjoy a Julia Bright novel.

Special Forces: Operation Alpha World

Christie Adams: Charity's Heart

Elizabella Baker: Challenging Luke

Linzi Baxter: Dangerous Rescue

Misha Blake: Flash

Anna Blakely: Rescuing Gracelynn

Julia Bright: Saving Lorelei

Cara Carnes: Protecting Mari

Kendra Mei Chailyn: Beast

Melissa Kay Clarke: Rescuing Annabeth

Gia Cobie: Saved from Revenge

Samantha Cole: Handling Haven

Cassie Colton: Rescuing Ryder

KaLyn Cooper: Spring Unveiled

Jordan Dane: Redemption for Avery

D.M. Earl: Claire's Guardian

Riley Edwards: Protecting Olivia

Dorothy Ewels: Knight's Queen

Lila Ferrari: Protecting Joy

Nicole Flockton: Protecting Maria
Lea Griffith: Finding Ava
Desiree Holt: Protecting Maddie
Danielle M. Haas: Crossroads of Betrayal
Bree Hera: Trusting the Team
Rayne Lewis: Justice for Mary
Kristin Lynn: Worth the Risk
JM Madden: Rescuing Olivia
A.M. Mahler: Griffin
Ellie Masters: Sybil's Protector
Trish McCallan: Hero Under Fire
Naomi McKay: Twist
KD Michaels: Saving Laura
Olivia Michaels: Protecting Harper
Annie Miller: Securing Willow
MJ Nightingale: Protecting Beauty
C.K. O'Connor: Delaney's Bodyguard
Danielle Pays: Defending Sarina
Lainey Reese: Protecting New York
Taryn Rivers: Savage Cove
TL Reeve and Michele Ryan: Extracting Mateo
Ariana Rose: Chasing Paige
Angela Rush: Charlotte
E.M. Shue: Discovering Tyler
Heather Slade: Code Name: Admiral
Dee Stewart: Fighting for Brielle

Lynne St. James: SEAL's Spitfire
Bella Stone: Rexar
Jen Talty: Protecting Ainsley
Reina Torres, Rescuing Hi'ilani
LJ Vickery: Circus Comes to Town
R. C. Wynne: Shadows Renewed

Delta Team Three Series
Lori Ryan: Nori's Delta
Becca Jameson: Destiny's Delta
Lynne St James, Gwen's Delta
Elle James: Ivy's Delta
Riley Edwards: Hope's Delta

Police and Fire: Operation Alpha World
Freya Barker: Burning for Autumn
B.P. Beth: Scott
Jane Blythe: Salvaging Marigold
Julia Bright: Justice for Amber
Gia Cobie: Saved from Revenge
Leyna Cohan: Embracing Juliette
Nicole Craig: Justice for Francesca
Danielle M. Haas: Crossroads of Betrayal
Deanndra Hall: Shelter for Sharla
India Kells: Game Master
Reina Torres: Justice for Sloane

Tarpley VFD Series

Silver James, Fighting for Elena

Deanndra Hall, Fighting for Carly

Haven Rose, Fighting for Calliope

MJ Nightingale, Fighting for Jemma

TL Reeve, Fighting for Brittney

Nicole Flockton, Fighting for Nadia

SEAL of Protection: Alliance Series

Protecting Remi
Protecting Wren
Protecting Josie
Protecting Maggie
Protecting Addison (May 6, 2025)
Protecting Kelli (Sept 2, 2025)
Protecting Bree (Jan 6, 2026)

Rescue Angels Series

Keeping Laryn (July 1, 2025)
Keeping Amanda (Nov 4, 2025)
Keeping Zita (Feb 10, 2026)
Keeping Penny (TBA)
Keeping Kara (TBA)
Keeping Jennifer (TBA)

The Refuge Series

Deserving Alaska
Deserving Henley
Deserving Reese

Deserving Cora
Deserving Lara
Deserving Maisy
Deserving Ryleigh

SEAL Team Hawaii Series

Finding Elodie
Finding Lexie
Finding Kenna
Finding Monica
Finding Carly
Finding Ashlyn
Finding Jodelle

Eagle Point Search & Rescue

Searching for Lilly
Searching for Elsie
Searching for Bristol
Searching for Caryn
Searching for Finley
Searching for Heather
Searching for Khloe

Delta Team Two Series

Shielding Gillian
Shielding Kinley

Shielding Aspen
Shielding Jayme (novella)
Shielding Riley
Shielding Devyn
Shielding Ember
Shielding Sierra

SEAL of Protection: Legacy Series

Securing Caite (FREE!)
Securing Brenae (novella)
Securing Sidney
Securing Piper
Securing Zoey
Securing Avery
Securing Kalee
Securing Jane

Delta Force Heroes Series

Rescuing Rayne
Rescuing Aimee (novella)
Rescuing Emily
Rescuing Harley
Marrying Emily (novella)
Rescuing Kassie
Rescuing Bryn
Rescuing Casey

Rescuing Sadie (novella)
Rescuing Wendy
Rescuing Mary
Rescuing Macie (novella)
Rescuing Annie

Badge of Honor: Texas Heroes Series

Justice for Mackenzie (FREE!)
Justice for Mickie
Justice for Corrie
Justice for Laine (novella)
Shelter for Elizabeth
Justice for Boone
Shelter for Adeline
Shelter for Sophie
Justice for Erin
Justice for Milena
Shelter for Blythe
Justice for Hope
Shelter for Quinn
Shelter for Koren
Shelter for Penelope

SEAL of Protection Series

Protecting Caroline (FREE!)
Protecting Alabama

Protecting Fiona
Marrying Caroline (novella)
Protecting Summer
Protecting Cheyenne
Protecting Jessyka
Protecting Julie (novella)
Protecting Melody
Protecting the Future
Protecting Kiera (novella)
Protecting Alabama's Kids (novella)
Protecting Dakota
Protecting Tex

New York Times, USA Today and *Wall Street Journal* Bestselling Author Susan Stoker has a heart as big as the state of Tennessee where she lives, but this all American girl has also spent the last fourteen years living in Missouri, California, Colorado, Indiana, and Texas. She's married to a retired Army man who now gets to follow *her* around the country.

www.stokeraces.com
www.AcesPress.com
susan@stokeraces.com

Made in the USA
Columbia, SC
15 June 2025

59440526R00126